I0606739

A Welcome War

War influences a young lad's
entire life…

Kev Richardson

A Wings ePress, Inc.

Historical Autobiography

Wings ePress, Inc.

Edited by: Karen Babcock
Copy Edited by: Jeanne R. Smith
Senior Editor: Pat Evans
Executive Editor: Marilyn Kapp
Cover Artist: Kathy Williams

All rights reserved

Wings ePress Books
www.wingsepress.com

Copyright © 2010 by Kevin Richardson
ISBN-13: 978-1-59705-512-3
ISBN-10: 1-59705-512-3

Published In the United States Of America

Wings ePress Inc.
3000 N. Rock Road
Newton, KS 67114

What They Are Saying About
A Welcome War

Multi-published historical writer **Kev Richardson** has a way of bringing the history of his homeland, Australia, up front and personal. In his latest work, **A WELCOME WAR**, I was notably impressed with his astute presentation of a young lad's impressions and compulsion to follow the happenings of World War II. From a ten-year-old's impassioned sense of wonder, to his later assessments as a young man of eighteen, he recounts his personal translation of the war that changed his life. The book includes many captivating memories from his younger years and his recorded impressions of the exciting historical happenings of war.

Kev Richardson presents his own bio as a schoolboy of ten confused by the changing colors on his war map, as countries continued to change hands during WWII. It became his first passionate effort to record history and the war that influenced the rest of his life. Yet **A WELCOME WAR** also gazes into the heart of a boy growing up to discover the pleasures of scouting, swimming, hiking... and girls... dancing, and kissing.

This account, which lists accurate dates and war-time impressions, verifies this writer's dedication to discovering and disclosing the truths in history that have in the past been purposely hidden. This enchanting biography of his own youth is not to be missed.

If you love history, I highly recommend you read all of Richardson's extensive historical writings about the First Fleet, and the men and women who populated the shockingly hidden history behind the penal colony in the beginning years of New South Wales, all available at www.wings-press.com.

5 Star Review!
JoEllen Conger
Conger Book Reviews, USA

Dedication

Truth exists. Only lies are invented.
George Braque

* * *

Preface

Dear Readers,

The Second World War was the most welcome and alluring war of all time.

It impacted on my life's goals more than any influence derived from education, family, or friends. That it instilled in my subconscious a penchant for history, geography, travel, and recounting life's adventures dawned on me when already into my eightieth year.

"Already, at eighty," you ask?

Well, it seems so.

My life since war's outbreak has continued ever-conscious of the influences then absorbed. Why else, I now question, have I continued to enjoy books and movies of that war's tales when I was seldom closer to its action than under the shielding canopy of childhood? However, the word 'seldom' must be considered appropriate in respect of two particular incidents—both when cannon-fire and explosions indeed impacted on my eyes, ears, and adrenalin. For the rest, however, it was simply desperate desire to be there rather than simply observing from afar.

Britons found peace returned when Germany surrendered, the Unites States didn't enter the actual fight until Britain had been at it two years, yet Australia was in the heat of conflict from the day Hitler *Blitzkrieged* his way into Poland until Japan surrendered several months after Germany. Trying to split straws is, of course, an unworthy exercise, yet youth chooses to look at things differently than those more experienced. From ages ten through sixteen, the war had immense impact on me. For what was to prove the most tellingly impressive period of my life, I was exposed to the world's geography, history, cultural differences, and political persuasions in the most colourful and adventurous medium any boy could hope to find. It beat schoolwork, hands down!

It was an extremely welcome form of education—welcome and alluring.

At the time, Australia was, and I even dare hint that more than a few people continue to insist that it remains, a land of frontier maturity.

When war erupted, Australia was the most isolated of 'western' societies. It might be one of the world's largest countries, yet at the outbreak of war, its population was but seven million, and the nearest 'western' civilisation, except for our Kiwi cousin, was half a world away in a time before air-transport. Its people could then afford neither the cost nor time of a five- to six-week journey afloat to reach Europe—with then the return journey to prolong the struggle.

Ninety-nine percent of Aussies had never travelled abroad.

An insular people?

Indeed—just as much as the remotest tribes of the Amazon!

I was eight years old when I first heard a foreign language. It was Chinese.

Awe and consternation, you might ask? Indeed, again.

I was being adventurous—a mate and I were skipping a different way home from school. We stopped because not only was there a loud verbal altercation in progress across a broad expanse of lavish garden, but we couldn't understand a word of it. We stared at each other in wonder, mouths agape, wondering if we'd somehow, without realising, left planet Earth to be instead, skipping along a detour on our way home via Mars. Never had such gabble assailed my ears—it left me so confused that I ran all the rest of the way to report my dilemma to Mum. I just hoped my sister was already home from school, so she could share my astounding adventure.

Into the hollow of the gentle hill where our house stood, water seeped from everybody's backyards such that nobody wanted to build 'down there.' Yet it was seemingly a swamp ideally suitable as a Chinese vegetable garden. I had never ventured in that direction when people were astir there, yet Mum would walk down the hill on occasions to buy what greens weren't in our own garden—and when I recounted my earth-shattering experience, she explained the cultural difference of people in the strangest of ways...

"Never put threepenny bits in your mouth," she told us, "because Chinese people put threepences in their ears."

My mind flew to the all the sorts of reasons why anybody would do such a thing, like to stop funnel-web spiders getting in, or some other sensible reason like that—but then came Mum's punchline: "And you must have noticed how dirty those people are!"

So what was my Mum really on about?

I'd got the clear message that she needed to illustrate the danger of putting tiny threepenny-bits in our mouths, okay, yet what did her closing sentence signify?

In fact, the typical Aussie attitude to foreigners was, back then, that they were misplaced in our midst. I now recognise that there was a conscious need to denigrate them when opportunity presented—like being a case of "we're all right, but every foreigner is suspect!"

Time was to prove that this was indeed the way dinkum Aussies saw outsiders.

After the war, the government realised how lucky we had been, escaping becoming a Japanese colony only because the Americans, with all their millions of men, joined the war. We were told that we must quickly populate the country or perish in the event of a future war. Displaced persons from war-ravaged European countries were invited to immigrate—which, having lost their all, they happily did; yet Australians en-masse made every one of them feel very much intruders. It took years of propaganda, cajoling—an entire generation in terms of time—before it was realised how much other cultures added to things we could enjoy, things like exotic tastes in food, fine wine, fashion, and even less insular ways of looking at things. We wanted to become part of the greater world all right, *yet only so long as we didn't have to mix with its strange people on our own turf!*

Only later did it become apparent that many even dinkum-bloody-Aussies had begun changing habits! Other cultures had persevered long enough to begin having a positive influence!

Or that's how it appeared to me as I grew.

However, that's getting ahead of things.

When the war came, everybody's life changed. This story is one account of what the war was to mean in the life of he too young to be in it, rather safe at home, yet nevertheless exposed to all the lies a government in wartime is obliged to feed its people—lies told rather than telling terrible truths. Secondly and more importantly, it was a time for people to ignorantly or maliciously begin rumours—reasons that during wartime were more numerous than can be imagined in peacetime.

Everyone seemed to be simply trying to change the order of things, and I couldn't work out why. All they were succeeding in, to my mind, was making life even more unexplainable.

An adage stuck in my mind over years is one by Bertrand Russell...

A stupid man's report on what a clever man says can never be accurate, because he unconsciously translates what he hears into something he can understand.

I've had that under a magnet on my fridge door for years.

It is relevant in the context of this tale, not so much stupid versus clever, but ignorant versus knowledgeable. The moral is the same and is certainly pertinent during wartime.

Whichever, ten-year-old kids had to make of rumour and propaganda what they might—all to be influenced by the results for the rest of their lives.

The following is a short burst of history about a dreadful time, yet a time to add unique irony in one who seemed to spend all of it with a genuine smile, if not visible on his face, at least causing a flutter just below the Adam's apple.

Kev Richardson

Glossary of Aussie Slang

Abo Australian Aborigine

Banana benders Queenslanders

Barbie Barbeque

Bloody Used by most Aussies as an adverb or adjective to lend either emphasis or empathy. It also serves, as an expression, as a sort of antidote to frustration.

Bonzer A considerable step-up from 'good'

Codger Old bloke

Cooee Distance of sound. That travelled by a bushman calling *Coooo-eee* and waiting for an echo if not an answer.

Dab A neat or clever hand at something

Damper Bushman's bread, made on hot coals with a stony rubble cover

Dinkum Alternative for *True Blue,* a tag to illustrate impeccably high value, such as an exceptionally worthwhile mate

Gob American sailor

Geyser see *Codger*

Humpy Primitive bush-hut

Jumper Woollen pullover, a Guernsey; 'jumper' being vernacular for a sheep

Larrikin Anyone behaving like a mischievous child

Midden Prehistoric refuse heap—in Australia, the physical discards of an Aboriginal feast

Swat Study, cram

Toey Rearin' to go!

Ute Vernacular for utility truck or pickup

Vegemite Breakfast spread on which Australians are weened. It addicts many throughout life. To be denied it occasions torturous withdrawal symptoms.

One

The Second World War was a tad longer for Aussies than for most.

The day after Hitler's Nazis began Germany's *Blitzkrieg* into Poland, Aussie queues at enlistment desks were as long as Britain's. Anzacs couldn't wait to be aboard ship, off to help save the world from Fascism.

I was ten years old and also ready to take on the world.

Mum and Dad were down-in-the-mouth about a war being declared.

We'd known it was coming, yet they'd hung on to the hope that a way around it might be possible. They'd been kids during the First World War and remembered it as a time of many deaths, of hardship and gloom for everybody. I hadn't seen such long faces in our house since Gypsy died.

Mum and Dad had then given the nod for, every Sunday since, Val and I to cut flowers from the garden to put on the mound under our mango tree. Never had there been a family loved a dog more, except maybe Mum when Gypsy dug holes in the garden or Dad when it was holes in the lawn. But the poor bitch had to bury her bones somewhere! Once we got her trained, however, they started loving her as much as Val and me. But this war thing started the gloom all over again.

Not for me, however. I was rapt. Here was real adventure in my life at last—not made-up stories from someone's imagination like Valerie and I saw at the flicks every Saturday—but real-live action for a kid to get stuck into.

"Where's this Poland place?"

Dad went straightway to his study where the Big Book, as I called the family atlas that answered most of my 'where' questions, had pride of place. Bookshelves lined an entire wall of Dad's study, and Dad reckoned he'd read every one. He opened the atlas on the breakfast-room table, again seeming to know, pretty closely, just where the page he needed would be. That skill, I'd ever admired.

We'd been listening to the wireless—usual at breakfast time. Mum and Dad always listened to the morning news with half an ear, yet now with this war breaking out, they were devouring every word. Their faces looked more shocked every minute—more shocked and more glum. I could see they considered it really important, almost as if it touched them personally.

I wanted to again ask, but could see now wasn't the time, why news from England always came early mornings—why big events in other countries always happened in the middle of the night when sensible people slept. All significant events in Australia seemed to happen during daytimes. But every time I asked, Dad seemed to change the subject. He'd take me to his study where the world globe stood, a coloured ball in a brass frame, tilted at a strange sort of angle I'd always reckoned. He'd start turning the globe around and, instead of answering my question, would begin a long tirade on how the earth keeps revolving. I could see that for myself, because he was pushing it. But once he stopped, it stopped.

"Well, as soon as you stop pushing it, Dad, it stops. So who's pushing the big world?"

And the lesson that would follow about how the earth and sun and moon are held up there by some mystic hand was ever beyond my ken. What all that had to do with events overseas being held at night rather than in the daytime never really got told until I joined the Boy Scouts. On my first camp we were taught how to tell the time by shadows, and only then did I start getting the gist of things. But it still seemed a strange thing for God to do—design a world that had a different time of day for everywhere else but where a body lived.

I'd already asked Ego, but he didn't know either.

I'd one time been told by Dad that I had, like every other soul, an alter-ego.

"It is the inner you," he would explain as if I knew what he was talking about. "It is the little person inside you that steers you along the right paths in life. You should always heed him."

So Ego was the one I would turn to when I couldn't get sensible reasons from adults. And I found he often seemed like a worthwhile friend. So I had to think about why, occasionally, he seemed to take my parents' side.

However, back to the Big Book on the breakfast table—Dad plopped his index finger on a purple patch.

"That's Poland, lad. It's a country in Europe, right next door to Germany, here." He moved his finger to a patch of green to the left of Poland.

Mum then tapped his arm.

"Please, Vic. I'm trying to listen to this!"

Dad pulled a face, gave a shudder as he grinned at me, and we all gave close attention to the wireless.

Val was older than me by two years. Most of my mates had sisters who were younger, so why my parents didn't have me first and then make the girl was a question I could never get answered either. Not even by Ego.

"It's because we never know in advance what the baby will be," had been Mum's response—yet another instance of an answer not being black or white.

Well all I can make of all this, I complained to Ego, *is that it's simply further evidence of never being able to get a question properly answered. It's like the pocket money sort of thing…*

"Never spend money on something you aren't sure of," she'd lecture us when we'd spent pocket money on some item she didn't approve of, or at least not see the value in it that we could.

It's not her money any more, is what would flash through my mind. *She gave it to me for my own pocket!*

Yet the fact she'd preach about us spending our money "on things you're not sure of," when she and Dad deliberately did the deed to make a baby without being sure what they were going to get, is what I reckoned was unfair. If ever I saw one, this was surely a case of preaching something they didn't practise—simply further evidence of the world being full of injustices.

Yet in the moment this war thing that was happening in the middle of last night had their minds so preoccupied that Dad wasn't even looking at his watch every few minutes to make sure he didn't miss his train. And it certainly wasn't a Sunday.

I twisted the atlas, still lying open, to better see what names were printed on the jumble of colours. 'Geography,' Dad called the study of maps, although to me every page was just a jumble of shapes and colours with names printed all over. And all was so formless, quite without any sort of design in the artist's mind like pictures in any other book.

"Every different colour is a different country," he'd once told me, as if that explained why it was a design so totally disorganised, entirely rhythm-less.

"Why is every country a different shape from others?" I would ask, but yet again I could never get a proper answer. I used to think he gave confusing answers to hide the fact that he didn't know, despite he never had a guilty look on his face, rather the same one as when helping me with homework.

However, I transfixed my mind on the fact that Germany was green and Poland purple. I tucked this information into the correct cranny of my mind should Mrs. Allison at school ask, "Who knows anything about these two countries?" I at least knew their colours.

So to me this was indeed a Welcome War, a whole new topic to hopefully put things like multiplication and spelling on the back-burner while we considered live action and adventure—aeroplanes, tanks, and Goodies and Baddies—real things to brighten life up.

~ * ~

Dad wasn't going off to war. Most schoolmates' fathers also decided, it seemed, to wait and see what would happen.

"They're conscripting eighteen-to-twenty-five-year-olds," Dad said. He was 'touching forty' as he put it. "And it's unlikely to be a long war. With modern aeroplanes, tanks, and fire-arms, things will likely be over quickly."

I asked why Germany was attacking Poland, to be told that that country had one time been part of Germany and many of its people were Jewish.

"And Germans don't like Jews," Dad explained.

Now neither was that the sort of answer to make lots of sense. Many kids at school I disliked so much that it was almost hate. But I wouldn't go charging into their houses belting everybody up. People I didn't like couldn't help being weird, so I just left them out of my life. There were always plenty of other kids around.

Mum said we should go to the pictures—that the newsreel would have all the action—but Dad reckoned we should wait. My dad had a mind like a Bondi tram: "If you don't keep it on the rails," he'd tell me, "you'll never get where you want to go."

He turned to Mum. "Movie-tone reels take a week or two to get here. With fighting now started, air schedules will be all over the place, even if not cancelled. Flights out of England will be controlled by military already, if my judgement's right." And his judgement mostly was, for he'd often enough told us so. "No more ten to twelve days for airfreight, I'd reckon. Anything to do with the war will have to go through censors first, so that could add many extra days."

Yet war didn't change things much around our district. From that very day I kept looking around, and it was mostly a matter of everybody still asking questions and not getting answers. I kept wondering what all the grown-ups were so jittery about. Trams were still running, Old Mrs. Gee's shop on the corner still had all the usual things on its shelves, teachers at school said things would start getting short, whatever that meant, but nothing seemed to make much difference to my life. I simply couldn't see what all the fuss was about.

A week later, however, I did get a shock. I was looking at the globe in Dad's study. I had found Europe and searched for Poland because the wireless had been talking again about the fighting there. They'd also talked about how the French expected little problem with the Germans attacking France like in the last war, because their Maginot Line, a string of forts built the entire length of the French border with Germany, was impregnable—built to keep France safe. I wanted to check out just where was the border they were talking about, but first things first...

Oh! Poland wasn't purple! It was yellow. And Germany, instead of being green like in the atlas, was a creamy sort of brown. It was France that was green. I took out the atlas and looked up the index for Europe—and there was no mistaking: Poland was purple, and Germany green. France was yellow.

What were they playing at? Which one was right, and which wrong?

I checked both the atlas map of the whole world, then the globe, and sure enough every nation of the British Commonwealth was red. Australia, Canada, India, Ceylon—which should be part of India too, I reckoned, because Tasmania was the same sort of offshore island on the Australian coast, and it was part of Australia—and there were New Zealand, South Africa, Rhodesia, Kenya, and Egypt... Yes, all British countries were coloured red on both atlas and globe.

But other countries were different. I quickly gave up, thoroughly confused. How could such oversights be made? Didn't anyone check their work before it went on the market?

That night I tackled Dad on the problem, but he didn't think it at all important. Nobody was obliged to use this or that colour for different countries, he insisted. It was a matter of everybody being free to colour any country as they pleased.

Yet somehow emblazoned on my memory was the fact that Poland should always be purple and Germany green. It had felt right—that that was how things should be. It was a settled sort of thing in my mind. I already tended to believe every purple-coloured product I sighted was Polish made, and everything green, except only the vegetables my mum and Chinamen grew, was German.

There really were some testy things involved when it came to education, I was beginning to realise.

No wonder, I reckoned, the world was in the terrible mess that Mrs. Allison kept reminding us of. With this sort of housekeeping in the homes of world organisers, I was beginning to get a measure of their poor proficiency.

Two

Some months later

Things had got a lot better. Germany was proving itself a thorough Baddie. Mum and Dad, Mrs. Allison, and everybody else who had been against the Germans from the outset had been proven right.

All except Mr. Atlee.

After the King, Mr. Atlee was boss of England, but the King didn't sit in Parliament, and Mr. Atlee did. He'd begun by saying Adolph Hitler wasn't all bad, that he wanted peace—but after attacking Poland, Hitler showed what sort of peace he'd meant. We kids at school had what we thought was a real clever piece of word-play on the subject: "Hitler wants peace, all right—piece of Belgium, piece of France, piece of Holland..."

His *Wehrmacht* and *Luftwaffe* had invaded and captured all those countries. And even before the war, he'd marched into Austria and Czechoslovakia. And very soon he was to add Denmark and Norway to his green list.

By now I'd coloured much of Europe green.

Sweden, Switzerland, Spain, and Portugal were the exceptions. They were countries that stayed neutral. I left them white in the map

I had traced so I had a map to write on, colouring things in as history changed.

We'd heard about the Soviet-Japanese War a long time ago, when I was young—too young to be bothered about it. And I wasn't alone. Most Aussies seemed to feel it was all so far away that it was no threat to us. We simply didn't care. And why should we?

After the real war started, Mr. Hitler openly attacked Jewish people living in Germany. These were the people Hitler didn't like. And he was really mean. One night he sent soldiers into the streets to destroy all the Jewish churches, Jewish shops, and Jewish homes. The damage was considerable. Then he stripped all of Germany's Jews of rights to attend theatre and cinemas and rounded up twenty thousand of them for imprisonment.

All the kids at school agreed with me—we were simply amazed at how many large gaols Germany must have.

Apart from Italy, Germany also had Russia as a friend, and when Germany invaded Poland from the west, Russia invaded it from the east—*Blitzkrieg* style is what they called it: tanks, military, and aeroplanes all charging at breakneck speed, killing anyone who got in their way, on the spot—and burning what they didn't believe worth saving. Exhibits from museums and art galleries, Dad read in the newspaper, were considered worth saving, so Hitler had all those sorts of things brought back to Germany for safekeeping. Russia at the same time marched into Finland, so you can imagine how much of my map I soon had coloured green.

I made much use of our atlas. I had promised not to write in it, but I could trace if I didn't press too hard. I made Mum and Dad promise to keep me up to date with any dramatic news they heard that I'd missed. But I was learning much about where these countries were, even to knowing the names of their capital cities.

Mrs. Allison, too, gave us daily talks on what she knew about each of these countries and reasons why Germany might want them—deep-water sea ports of which Germany had few, coal-mines and oil-wells of which Germany also had too few, but most of all, Mrs. Allison said, what they really wanted to accumulate was power.

"And power can be used for evil as well as good," she reckoned.

She made it pretty clear that she had Germans well and truly in her 'Baddies' category, yet I at least had them as heroes at winning. Baddies or not, they beat every other country hands down at fighting. They were really good at that.

Then one day on the wireless, I was chucked a real teaser—one to send me quickly scurrying for the big dictionary.

"Collateral damage," the announcer called the people jamming French roads, trundling their treasured belongings from bombed houses, threading their ways between tanks and columns of trucks trying to get big guns to the safety of the west. Nazi Stukas were dive-bombing the columns, of course. So it was clear that 'collateral' had everything to do with the unlucky people who were simply getting in the way.

I wrote that word down. It would be a telling one to use when writing up my diary.

Val and I were used to crawling into bed with Mum and Dad every Sunday. Dad would bring in the newspaper that got tossed over the fence from the dickie-seat of the newsagent's roadster—breaking Mum's poppies more often than not, she would continue to complain to the newsagent—and read the news to us. When he'd finished the war news, he would turn to the comics; that's when Mum would put on her gown and go to start breakfast.

Dad told me about his private thoughts on war things closer to home. He was worried about Japan.

"Japan has long been at war against China and seems to be winning," he said. "Their biggest problem is having too many people for such a small country"—we looked this up in the atlas also. "It has not enough land to grow rice, their staple food."

He explained how they had no space for grazing animals like sheep and beef.

Well, that turned me against Japan straight off. Any place with no meat that Mum put on our table three meals a day wouldn't suit me at all. Yet it didn't matter, because when I said I hoped Dad's work wouldn't transfer him there next, he assured me that that would never happen.

"But they won't be satisfied with China," he told me. "Japan is industrialised but has no raw materials. They buy coal and pig iron from us, petrol from the US and the Dutch East Indies, and foodstuffs from just about everybody. They'll get lots more rice from China after their war there, but raw materials for their factories is another matter. In the long term they will want more lands. Malaysia has big deposits of tin, and Burma has many mineral resources."

Dad would always scoot us off then. Sunday was his day for fixing things around the house or gardening.

"...To feed you kids," he would say. "The more quickly you grow big and strong enough to do more work in the garden, boy, is the only reason I feed you, you know."

I would look to see if his face had a grin on it. But it never did.

When he said things like that while looking so serious it always gave me guilty shivers up the backs of my legs. Val and Mum would reckon he was joking. But I was never sure.

~ * ~

Val and I went to Windsor State School, a two-mile walk each way, but we didn't mind because we every day made the journey with other kids. It was best of the government schools in Brisbane is what Dad was told when we moved from Sydney. All private schools had waiting lists 'as long as one's arms,' his friends reckoned.

But we were happy with it. Being Brisbane's only school with a swimming pool gave it bonus points in my book. And it had huge grounds. And the tuck-shop over the road from the 'top' gate had the best steak pies with mashed peas that a kid ever tasted. Pies were tuppence, and a scoop of peas a penny. On a shelf by the door was a bottle of Worcester sauce that you could shake on for free, and I reckoned that any shop that gave kids anything for free was great 'thumbs-up-stuff.' We both were given fourpence each day—threepence for lunch and a penny for an ice-block to nibble in the heat of Queensland sun during our walk home. I found queuing up for lunch every day nearly as exciting as having the war for my hobby. That daily pie'n-peas was to remain in my memory for many a year.

Val was in her all but last year at primary school, and Dad was already working on what was best available as a girls' high school. Some were starting to teach business subjects for girls, and he reckoned something in that line might be right for Val.

But it's a long way off yet, was all I could feel about it. This year was only three months old, so there was plenty of time to worry about boring stuff like that. My opinions, however, seldom got much attention at home, especially now Mum was so touchy about the war—trying to organise her cooking around rationing and worrying over when Dad might get called up to be sent away. I told Dad that if he did get called up, he should sign on as a general so he could still be a boss like at work. And he said he might just try that.

We had to have coupons now for many kinds of food as well as clothing. I made no comment about Val's schooling nor mine, because high school for me was three years off—a lifetime away. But another great adventure arrived out of the blue...

Easter school holidays had started, longest annual break except for the six-week summer break over Christmas. Dad was away on business. His company's Adelaide office had a problem, and it was in Dad's 'area of expertise' as he put it, so he had been shipped off to Adelaide for as long as it took him to fix it. There were no made roads south of Brisbane except for some fifty of the seven hundred miles to Sydney and then maybe another fifty on the 'track' from there to Adelaide—a thousand miles of dust and sand, that stretch was, he said. There were no sleeping cars on trains so he went by ship, ten to twelve days each way. Val had already gone by train to Sydney, where Uncle Harold, one of Dad's brothers, only one with a motor car, was taking her to Melbourne for a holiday. He and Aunt Olive were going there on business. It was too far to drive on mud roads, so they would go by train and stay in the plush Chevron Hotel. Val was highly excited.

Harold and Olive had no children and had adopted Val as a sort of 'surrogate' daughter, whatever that meant. So after she'd left, Mum and I had the house to ourselves until Ashley Wright drove up to our door one day in a brand new motor car. Now this might be a bit confusing so I'll work up to it slowly...

Ashe worked in Townsville, more than a thousand miles north of Brisbane, so we were more than a bit surprised to see him. His car was not big—a little wire-wheeled Austin sedan.

"G'day, Ame," he said to Mum as if he'd known her all her life although they'd only met once. Mum's name is really Amy—AmyMay—but she got 'Ame' from family and friends and Ashe was, well, 'sort' of family; this is the tricky bit... His wife Merle was daughter of Mum's aunt. Yes. My grandma on Mum's side was one of seventeen kids all born in Tasmania, where Mum was born even before that aunt. One day about six months prior, Mum got a telegram from Merle and Ashe, although she'd never met them, to say they would be in Brisbane next week. They were travelling from Tassie all the way to Townsville in North Queensland, to live—all the way by ship. When taking a week stay-over in Sydney to meet family, Merle was told that she now had an aunt living in Brisbane, so Merle wanted to meet Mum. Mum had only been six years old when leaving Tassie. Her father had got a job in New South Wales.

Are you still with me on all that?

Well, we met Merle and Ashe when their ship came to Brisbane. They had to wait three days before sailing on to Townsville. They were nice people, and Mum got lots of news from the few relatives she could remember in Tassie. Merle and Ashe then sailed off for the north, and we'd not heard of them since.

Now here was Ashley on our doorstep.

"Merle went off to Tassie, Ame," he told Mum, "and when I wrote to tell her I planned to drive down to see her, the Townsville Austin dealer sponsoring my trip, she answered that I should ask you if you wanted a lift as far as Sydney to see your sisters. But you'll have to train it back."

He rattled all that off as if it were simply the time of day he was talking about.

Now my mum for all her life had been an organised lady. She had always done her own housework, same as most women in those times, and her home was always in impeccable condition—sort of scrubbed with fervour every morning and curtains laundered every other day in case the Queen should decide to pop in for a cuppa. Even the kitchen biscuit caddy was always stocked with fresh cookies against such an event... oh, and there was always a spare jar of Vegemite, just in case the Queen wanted to try a taste of real Aussie food. And Mum loved to organise other people as well as she did her house. She seemed to see it a public duty. She certainly organised me from the moment I popped. At a very early age, I realised that a kid's life was nowt more than what Dad called 'a course in defensive realism.' He always had a smile on his face as he said that, I noticed.

But I learned to parry Mum's organising abilities, swing with the punches, yet I'd never had opportunity to see her mind in action as on this occasion.

What did she answer to Ashe?

"Oh! I shall need to cancel the newspaper deliveries, tell Mrs. Gee I will not be requiring milk every day, ask Mrs. Cook next door to water my poppies, pin a note to the door for the ice-man, write to..."

Then she faltered.

"...and I shall have to ask someone to take Kevin in. Would you really ask me to do that? Leave my son alone here when his sister is in Melbourne and his father in Adelaide?"

Poor Ashley looked dumbfounded.

"I hadn't realised Vic was away," he answered. "Nor Valerie. But Kevin can come with us if you like."

I was starting to feel like a ping-pong ball in a rally.

"Well, that's settled," was Mum's response, the glimmer of a smile on her lips.

Wow! Here was I invited to take the journey of a lifetime—a motor car journey to Sydney! Had any kid in Australian history ever done such?

And suddenly my brain was in a whirl—but what about the war?

I knew it wouldn't stop if I missed news broadcasts or with Mum putting the newspaper subscriptions on hold, yet I might well miss out on something significant—like another country being overrun. Suddenly I was conscious that maybe I'd inherited Mum's organising ability...

"But, Uncle Ashe, what about petrol? Don't you need coupons?"

"Forget the 'Uncle' tag, Kev… coming from a grown boy like you, it makes me feel old. And there's no worry about coupons, my sponsor's given me a bagful. Would you like to come?"

Oh, what a great guy Ashe suddenly became.

"Wouldn't I ever!"

~ * ~

The Austin had four doors and a running board both sides, the rear half of each stacked high with a leather suitcase tied on with rope.

"I've two bags, Ame, for I'll be away several months. Just as well you are going only a fraction of my distance. Your luggage can fit on the back seat alongside Kev."

I knew what he didn't.

Overnight, Mother, after writing her several letters and neighbour notes, packed three large suitcases, two hatboxes, several canvas bags stashed with everything spoilable from the ice-chest including salads and leftovers from last-night's dinner, eggs from the hen-house, and a large shopping basket with all the fruit from our sideboard, bottles of home-made lemonade, cakes and biscuits, and an entire quarter of ham she had taken delivery of from Mrs. Gee only two days ago. She'd even gone out into the garden and plucked anything getting near ripe—mangoes, paw-paws, and a pumpkin. I had my school-port with my notebooks for recording the progress of the war.

When Ashe arrived at five o'clock next morning, mother had all stacked into a sort of tower by the front gate—an impressive pile indeed. She was happily tapping the minutes away, hoping Ashe would be on time. I was still trying to wake up.

I had the feeling that Ashe didn't dare suggest she was bringing too much; he was too much the gentleman. He simply began loading, taking his own luggage from the running board because two of Mother's three were portmanteau size. They were strapped on the running boards blocking off both back doors, and Mum's front door could open only a little—but enough for her to wriggle in with difficulty. The rest were wedged into the back, right up to the roof.

On the roof he had two more spare wheels, a shovel, Hessian bags in case we were stuck in mud, a box of tools, and a four-gallon can of spare petrol. On the back of the car, where larger models had a luggage compartment, hung the regular spare wheel and a smaller box with tyre-changing equipment.

Mum scoffed. "Well, I hope we won't be needing the shovel and those sacks."

Ashe but smiled. He whispered to me, while she was dusting the seat she had to sit on, that he had had to change a wheel on the journey from Townsville on four occasions.

To gain my seat in back, just enough space between the pile of luggage and the door to fit me if I didn't breathe too deeply, I had to get in through Mum's door, then clamber over the back of her seat. From there it was only an awkward tumble into mine.

The sun rose as we exited Brisbane on the road to Beaudesert and the mountains that stretched along the New South Wales-Queensland border.

I had never felt so confined in my life. It was extremely bumpy, and I had the back doorhandle pressing into my elbow on my right unless I kept my arm across my body rather than let it rest at my side. The luggage on my left was so copious it gave me not an inch of movement. Ashe had been careful to leave as much space for me as he could. *But,* I mused, *how lucky I am that I'm not a fat kid like Boswell at school.* When Boswell went into the swimming pool, it was instantly like high tide at Sandgate.

The Mount Lindsay Highway, only road south over the New South Wales border, was extremely winding, and when heavy black clouds not only appeared before us but proceeded to descend right on top of us, Ashe was worried.

"If as much rain falls as these clouds seem to threaten, Ame, it will make it damned difficult to drive. The road will turn to slush, and in these mountains, with our load, it will be a slow trip. In heavy rain, mud roads get slippery on the edges."

I peered down from the only window I could see out of; there were no fences. Only careful driving could stop us going over into the ravine if we began a slide.

"Is there somewhere we can stop until the weather clears?"

"Nothing shows on the map, Ame."

"Then we shall simply have to stop on the roadside and wait."

"I don't know that we'll have time to stop. We must make Tenterfield by nightfall. However, we don't need to consider that until we see what happens with the weather. It may pass."

It didn't. It waited only long enough for Ashe to finish speaking.

And there was another problem. My tummy was feeling squeamish. I'd never driven a long distance in a motor car, and Mother had pre-conditioned me with the information that some people get ill riding in the back of a car on mountain roads.

Now, was I feeling ill only because she had warned me about it?

But my tummy certainly was giving me messages. Mum had already spread brown paper over my stomach as I dressed—"It will deter 'travel-sickness'," she said. But my stomach hadn't been listening. I tried keeping my eyes on the road so I would have some warning of a curve coming up, but with the rain, it was too difficult to see much. Ashe had the wipers going, but they weren't strong enough to clear the mud. I hoped we didn't find a car coming the other way, because the road was very narrow.

Then I had to think how many cars travelling north had passed us.

One. It was while we had stopped in a straight stretch for Ashe to eat his sandwich lunch. There had been many cars on the Brisbane streets, but once we had left the city, there had been only that one.

"I shall never forget how seasick I was when, as a six-year-old, we sailed from Tassie to Newcastle," Mum was saying to Ashe. "And when we moved from Sydney to Brisbane, I was sick again."

I remembered that. I was only six when my family moved interstate. Dad had gone by train to become Queensland Manager, Mum staying behind with Val and me to arrange shipping of furniture and to quit the house. We sailed to Brisbane on the steamer *Westralia* because there were no sleeper trains and the train, with all the stops, took some twenty hours. The ship was two nights and three days, and Mum was sick all the way. But what an adventure for me! Val sat with

Mum mostly, but I went exploring. Many times I got lost. Mum then had Val safety-pin a note on my shirt with my name and our cabin number on it.

I distinctly remember the time I didn't get lost...

~ * ~

"Now do you remember the way to the dining room?" Mum asked when I was off for the first time on my own for a meal.

I probably nodded.

"And do you remember the people at our table? Will you know them again if you look for them?"

I think I nodded again. I remembered one lady was fat, with white hair, ripply skin, and a pink dress. I found the dining room by following other people, yet when I looked, I couldn't see a fat lady in a pink dress. But I did see a spare chair at a table. One man wore a smart white uniform with gold braid on its sleeves. I pulled out the chair and sat in it. Everybody at the table laughed, and the man in uniform, who told me he was the captain, read my tag.

"You are welcome, Kevin," he said, and everybody talked to me all the time through lunch. When the captain asked me what I wanted to eat, I told him meat pie and peas, and everyone laughed again. They didn't have pies, so I had a jam sandwich and fried potato chips with ice-cream. After lunch one of the ladies took me back to our cabin and talked with Mum, who must have been feeling better, for she even laughed.

Dad was waiting for us at the wharf when we arrived after breakfast on the third day. That journey had been an adventure I shall never forget.

The *Westralia* was converted to a troop carrier during the war.

~ * ~

However, on that winding road, I was suffering like Mum on the ship.

Behave! I told Ego, hoping he had influence on my stomach—but either he didn't, or it hadn't listened.

Without warning my belly erupted, and oh, did I ever spew! Up it came all over me, the car seat, the floor, and the pockets built inside the door for things like books or sandwiches (but obviously not spew). My flailing arms, no doubt flailing in instinctive desire to quell the eruption, broke the string holding back the pile of luggage so that it tumbled all over me, the seat, and the spew.

~ * ~

"Why is it so important getting to Tenterfield by nightfall?"

"Because, Ame, newspapermen will be waiting. Since Townsville I have been tied to what my sponsor considered a reasonable day's run. So everything is booked, and I am to be met by reporters at every overnight, the entire three thousand miles to Tassie. Do you realise that you are part of the longest motor car journey ever in the history of Australia? And I have to do it in three weeks."

My sick ears pricked at that. "This, then, is a real adventure for you too, Ashe? One to send trembles through you?"

He leaned across to pat a hand on my knee, me now sitting in Mum's lap. There was no longer space for me in the back. Ashe hadn't wanted to spend the time re-stacking the luggage; he'd stopped only long enough for Mum to sponge me and everything else down with tea from the thermos, without getting out in the torrential rain. She carried cleaning cloths in her purse, of course.

"I keep them for cleaning soot off train seats when we're going to the city," my ever-organised mum explained.

"Yes, lad," Ashe answered. "It is indeed adventure. When we get to Sydney, ask your mum to get you the week's issues of the *Sydney Morning Herald*. You can read what they've written about us. And there'll be photos for your scrapbook. They're running a daily serial on me. After Sydney it's to be the *Melbourne Age* and *Hobart Mercury*." He explained how, from Melbourne, he would take the car across the strait to Tasmania in an overnight ferry.

Wow! Adventure indeed! As was our arrival in Tenterfield, where several photos of Ashe and the car were taken.

I had never stayed in a hotel, but *The Royal* in rural Tenterfield was the town's biggest—and luckily so because while they had rooms for Ashe and all the reporters in town, they had to do some reshuffling to find a room for Mum and me. Mum reckoned someone less important had to sleep under the kitchen table.

We were late arriving, but the oven had been kept alight for us and they served up roast mutton with mint sauce and some of the best roast potatoes I'd ever had. Mum gave me a sly look when they served spinach. She knew I didn't like it, but she also knew I would recognise her sly look if I left it. I ate it all without problem because not only was my stomach better now, having been out of the mountains for the past few hours during which the rain had petered out, but I reckoned eating something I didn't particularly like was small payment for the excitement of the occasion.

We were up at five thirty next morning, and Mum had me help her in the empty kitchen to make fresh tea for the thermos and to cut and spread sandwiches, some with Vegemite and some with tomato and the ham she'd brought with us. Come breakfast, by which time a cook had arrived, I asked if there was a wireless to give me news of the war.

"Our radio gets beamed from Armidale, lad. But we won't get news from outside until midday. You won't get city services along this road."

So I had to be content to wait for war news at some future stop.

But, oh dear! Some ten miles south of Tenterfield, having filled up with petrol and had the car given the once-over overnight by the town mechanic, we had our first real problem. Twice already since starting the day's journey, Ashe and I had had to get out and move rocks off the track for a clearer path through. With small stones, of which there were plenty, we crossed fingers that the tyres would best them. And so far they had. But this time we heard nowt unusual, but the car started to tremble in a funny way.

"Bloody puncture," said Ashe.

He told Mum to stay in the car. "But you can help me fix this, Kev."

But Mum wanted to stretch her legs. The morning was fine, and the sun was yet mild.

"I've been counting the miles since we left this morning," she told us as I helped Ashe get a shod wheel from the roof, pestered by more bush-flies than even at a barbie.

"Why's that, Ame?"

"I lived near here as a girl. My family left Tassie when I was six because my father had been appointed manager of the Emmaville Tin Mine."

"The turn-off to Emmaville is just down the road apiece according to the map," said Ashe.

"Yes. That's the signpost I'm looking for."

"I doubt we'll have time to go see the town…"

"I don't want to go there, Ashe. Five years we lived there, and that was the worst time of my life."

Ashe waited as we worked, me helping once he showed me how to wind up the jack. But she never said any more. I knew my mum had been born into a tin-mining family. Her grandfather owned the pub on Tassie's Blue Tier, where its Anchor Mine became the biggest tin-mine in the world at the turn of the century. The grandpa I never knew, because he died about the time I was born, had brought his family, including Mum, to New South Wales when the tin started to run out in the Blue Tier. But I hadn't known it was this part of the world that she came to.

In fact it wasn't until after her death at a respectably old age that Val and I learned what a wretched childhood she had had after leaving Tassie. It was a time of her life she would never talk about.

And she illustrated by her silence as Ashe and I continued working that she wasn't going to talk about it then, either.

Three

Back at Windsor State I was man of the moment. Mrs. Allison told me the headmaster wanted to see me. My heart skipped—a 'what did I do wrong?' kind of skip.

"You are the only boy in this school who has ever travelled so far by motor car," she told me. "The head wants to talk to you about it."

Wow! And this the biggest school in Brisbane! I was more nervous than ever I'd been. But he wasn't scary. He asked how long it had taken and what were the experiences that I found most inspiring and things like that. He told me he'd never been to Sydney, and that made me feel extra tall.

Mrs. Allison then told me she wanted me to take the floor during class and tell all the kids about it. "Give it some thought overnight," she said, "then we can do it first thing tomorrow."

My head whirled.

Mum and Dad had plenty of suggestions about the sorts of things I should say, and Dad showed me how to make reminder notes to keep in my palm, sort of what I should talk about in turn—things that would interest the whole class rather than just my special friends. So I had plenty of thinking to do once abed that night.

Three weeks I'd been away. The drive down was three nights on the road—oh, with so many stops to change wheels. On the second day we had punctures in all three spares, and I helped Ashe take out the tube and make a patch, then pump up the tyre again. He had a service station mend all the punctured tyres over each night. It was only once that we had to make the patch. Luckily it held okay. We had travelled high mountain roads with sheer drops down one side or the other, and we'd had to ford little rivers, hoping the water wouldn't get into the exhaust pipe. We often saw motor cars on the track on both near and far sides of towns but, in open countryside, practically never. Only five cars passed us the entire trip, and we passed only one—that gives you some idea of how lonely Australian roads could be. How many times I had to get out and move rocks off the road ahead, however, I lost count. That had become my special role. Every time we came into a steep gully area with walls up one side, there were fallen rocks, some so big Ashe had to come and help me. In the entire trip I saw twice as many rocks as even kangaroos. Mum nursed me through the constant motion-sickness all the way, uncomplainingly. I tried not to wriggle too much.

We stayed with Aunty Ida—one of those 'aunties' who wasn't a real aunt but my mum's best friend ever, even her bridesmaid. We visited all Mum's sisters and Grandma many times. Mum telephoned Uncle Harold at his hotel in Melbourne to tell him we were in Sydney. They were to leave next day, so he would deliver Val to Aunt Ida's instead of putting her on the train for Brisbane. And Dad's work told Mum when she phoned them that his steamer was due in the following Saturday— so we waited the extra days so we all could train home together. Wow! Had I ever seen so much of my country?

It certainly had been Adventure with a capital 'A.'

~ * ~

Dad's gift for me for having behaved during his absence was my first ever pair of long trousers. I felt something like the prime minister when I looked in the big mirror. So I wore them when addressing the class. Boy! Did I ever get some ribbing! I was the only kid in class to own a pair of long trousers.

"Kids are wearing them younger in Sydney," I told them, unsure if it were a truth or a government-type lie.

But life was pretty good for me these days, and I'd learned that worry never got a kid anywhere. This was especially borne out one time when I'd been learning, for a while, to play the piano. Dad had given one to the whole family for the Christmas after arriving in Brisbane, and Mum and I were the ones to take to it. Val and I then learned that she could play by ear. Mum would simply hear a tune, and with a few minutes' practise, away she'd go, playing as if she'd been playing it all her life. And she couldn't read a note. So I wanted to be like that, too. 'Aunt' Olive Dinte, a really big, fat lady who lived next door, could play the piano pretty good, and she was teaching me. My big chance in life came up when Mum put my name down at the local church Family Musical Evening. Wow! I was actually to play before an audience. Now my usual style was that when I'd learned to play a piece by reading the music, I'd tend to forget to watch the sheet music and watch my fingers so they wouldn't make a mistake. Well, that night I played "The Blue Danube Waltz," and I don't know what my mind must have been wandering on, for all I knew was that I had, by then, no idea where was my place on the sheet music, and I couldn't remember what came next.

But my mind did remember that big Olive Dinte would say to me when I'd mucked something up: "Well, it's not the end of the world, dear, let's simply start again." So that night, that's what I did. And I reckon nobody even noticed, for when I'd finished, everyone still clapped.

On Saturday afternoons, Val and I would walk the fourteen blocks to the flicks at The Grange. We seldom went to the Wilston Flicks. It was closer to home, but because it was an open-air theatre they couldn't operate in the rain—and never at night now, of course, with the blackouts. The Grange cinema had an upstairs, and every Saturday afternoon we went to see the News of the World and follow the Flash Gordon serials, followed by whatever picture was on. We were each given seven pence for the occasion, sixpence for entry and a penny for an ice-block at interval. Val would meet her boyfriend, Cookie, there, and he would slip me a penny by way of bribe to sit downstairs while he and Val sat upstairs. I had to promise not to tell Mum or Dad, but I kept the secret. I saw it a challenge—like the spies in Europe had to cope with.

If they can do it, I told Ego, *so can I.*

I knew it was all right to keep secrets from people because Mum used often to remind me not to tell anything about the family to old Mrs. Gee at the corner shop. Mum reckoned Mrs. Gee saved up gossip to tell every other customer.

But at the flicks I'd wait out front when all was finished so Val and I could walk home together. Cookie would walk with us and other friends until we got to the corner near our house. Then he'd cross the road in case our dad was home from tennis to see him with us. Dad put the garden hose on Cookie one time.

~ * ~

The war hadn't waited for me to get back from Sydney. It hadn't been easy at Aunt Ida's or any relative we visited because there was always chit-chat going on, noisy at that with lots of laughing, as if they weren't going to be seeing each other again for "God knows how long," as they called it.

If I asked could I listen to a wireless, I'd only find that all stations were different from Brisbane, and I never knew which one to pick; newspapers I looked at had worse news than even Brisbane papers. Once home, however, I found that Germany was sitting pretty with all Europe neatly wrapped up and was now landing troops in the north of Africa. It just seemed that they were never going to be satisfied.

Bloody Hell, I reckoned. I didn't mind swearing because I just felt so annoyed. The Germans had prepared themselves well for this war. They'd made no attempt to hide from anyone that they were arming, yet it seemed no other nation, absolutely none, had done much by way of getting ready. Even I could see how easy it seemed for every nation to be caught with their pants down.

Prime Minister Menzies was worried that there were so many Aussie men clamouring to be sent overseas, same as in the last war, that if he sent troops to help England beat the Germans, Australia would find itself batting on a sticky wicket if Japan decided to turn on us when all our troops were on the other side of the world. Dad reckoned that could well be on the cards. Mr. Menzies told England we would send only volunteers to Europe. Conscripts would have to stay to defend Australia. England asked him to send the volunteers to Egypt to guard the Suez Canal. Mr. Menzies sent twenty thousand.

It was a pretty good thing, I reckoned, when Mr. Churchill became prime minister of Great Britain. Mr. Atlee had let Hitler really pull the wool over his eyes. Even I could tell Mr. Churchill was a man of solid guts. It was him organised every little fishing boat in the south of England to whip across to France to lift the British army boys off the beach at Dunkirk before the Germans could take them all prisoner.

I had got the feeling that the English Channel was something a bit like the Brisbane River, only wider, yet Dad reckoned it was even more. We got out the atlas, and Dad showed me how to work out how many miles from the little graph on every page. He was right again, of course. It certainly was wider than the Brisbane River, by more than twenty times.

Italy had seized the British island of Malta in the Mediterranean while I was away, then come August it occupied British Somaliland, and in September invaded Egypt.

Japan by now controlled all of Korea, Manchuria, and Mongolia and most of China's coastline, its southern states, and the island of Formosa. French Indo China that comprised the old countries of Vietnam, Cambodia, and Laos now came under the banner of the Vichy French, as did Mauritius, the Seychelles, and Madagascar in the Indian Ocean. Seemingly the whole world was being swallowed up by the Axis Bloc. If I'd thought Mum and Dad had had long faces at the start of the war, they were now even longer.

Dad said Japan had its eyes on the oil-rich Dutch East Indies and that those islands were starting to look like sitting ducks for the Japs with now no Dutch government in power to protect them.

"And once they've got those," Dad said, "it's just a matter of a few island stepping-stones to Australia."

I looked all that up on the big globe and it certainly did seem to be that way.

Things were not looking good at all.

~ * ~

One day, Dad and I were in a tram going somewhere when a car pulled up at a kerb across the road—it was an Austin, bigger model than Ashe's little sedan and a silvery sort of colour, with extra-smart curves.

"What do you think of that for a car, eh?"

"Very nice," I answered.

"Well, that's the one I'm looking at. You reckon you'd be happy if we had one of those under the house?"

My heart jumped. None of my mates had a car in their family, except one whose father was a builder and had a ute. I knew my dad was good at his job and Mum had told us kids a while back that he'd been given a good raise.

However, about that time things on our home front started to sour rather than get better—and I don't mean the war front. Dad was getting bad headaches, and it was unlike him to be sick. We had always been a healthy family except when I'd come down with a disease just after moving from Sydney. I was rushed to hospital to be put in an isolation ward once they diagnosed diphtheria. It was so widespread in our part of Brisbane that they closed our school for several months. But hospital proved a pretty good place; just like a holiday it was for me, because all I was given to eat was ice cream. How better could things get than that?

Dad wasn't so lucky. Mum started asking me to do more things around the garden to save him, and I knew he was seeing lots of doctors. Mum never said much to us kids—it was only later that we realised that she reckoned it would only cause us extra worry. Val and I talked about it, of course. We knew something wasn't right because he was starting to act strange at times—like suddenly losing the track of what he'd been talking about. One day when we arrived home from school—late, because we boys had taken a detour to raid an old witch's loquat tree while the girls waited—we found Dad had been taken to hospital. And he never came out. He was diagnosed with a brain tumour, and there was nowt doctors could do.

"It's a cancer in the brain, and you can't operate on the brain," they told Mum. "Even if he were the King, there's nothing we can do. It's just a matter of waiting."

Mum didn't tell us that part—but she certainly kissed and cuddled us kids more than ever. She telephoned Uncle Harold, and he and Dad's sister Moogs, real name Muriel but affectionately called Moogs by the wider family, came by the next day's train.

Dad died within days of that, and things were all pretty hectic.

Aunt Moogs told us that Dad's oldest sister, Aunt Estelle, would also have come except she now lived in India, a missionary. I went with Uncle Harold over the road to Mrs. Gee's shop so he could telephone Sydney. After that, of course, we didn't have to tell anybody in our entire suburb about Dad dying—Mrs. Gee took care of that.

Uncle took Val and me in a taxi to school to tell our teachers we were going to Sydney and wouldn't be back. I was told to pack up all my things—clothes and all my notes, my scrapbook and maps of the war.

At the funeral were all Dad's workmates, friends from the church Bridge Club where Mum and Dad played two nights a week, and friends from the Tennis Club where they played every Saturday while Val and I were at the flicks.

I'd never seen a dead person, but the casket was open for all the family to kiss him. Two days later, Val and I left on the train with Moogs and Harold. Mum stayed to settle up the house and arrange furniture and things to be shipped back to Sydney. Uncle needed to get home quickly because he was booked to sail for England on business—something about changes because of the war, and he had many things to finalise before leaving. He and Aunt Olive used to visit England every three or four years. She was English anyway and had family in Yorkshire, which was where most of his cutlery and tool business colleagues were. Aunt Olive wasn't going with him this time, however, because of the war.

What Val and I didn't know as we boarded the train was that Uncle had Dad's ashes packed into his luggage. They were to be buried in their mother's family mausoleum in Sydney's Waverly Cemetery.

"He'll be happier buried with his mother in Sydney where you'll be able to visit, rather than be left on his own in Brisbane," we were later told.

"That will be Mum's organising again," I told Val.

And oh, how our family's life changed then. It had all been so quick—and not enough time to properly say goodbye to friends.

Until Mum finished sorting out all involved in quitting Brisbane and then organising accommodation in Sydney, Val would live with Aunty Moogs and I would live with Uncle Eric, Dad's nearest brother in age, not too far from Val. Mum's family and Dad's families were all Sydney-based, so it was pointless her staying on alone in Brisbane. All our family branches lived on the North Shore, so it was agreed before leaving that it was somewhere there that Mum would seek accommodation.

~ * ~

The war didn't even stutter over all this, of course.

I rued the lack of Dad's good foresight in respect of Japan's intentions, for it seemed he'd been right on the ball. Japan marched into Indo China on the very day he died. Later I discovered that it had signed an alliance with Germany and Italy to become a fully-fledged member of the Axis Bloc. From that very day, Japan was at war with Australia, distant Canada, gem-rich India, Ceylon, Burma, Malaysia, the Pacific's biggest port Singapore—and the oil-rich Dutch East Indies. Only the neutral Kingdom of Thailand, recently renamed from Siam, stood in Japan's way of attacking Burma and Malaya overland.

Japan offered Thailand a non-aggression pact if given land access to Burma (en-route to India) and Malaya (en-route to Singapore). Thailand had never been colonised. It was proud of that unique label, the only nation in the largest continent in the world with independence to protect—so it was a pretty easy decision for it to take. It would have been suicidal not to accept.

Movie-tone newsreels were coming thick and fast into Australia now. Every week at the flicks, although I couldn't get to a cinema as frequently now, news of the war was there in black and white for all to see—and the camera never lied, of course. German Stukas had dive-bombed roadways in France, machine-gunning every thing that moved. It was vivid stuff, all right, and the Baddies were really playing it dirty.

"But surely it cannot last long," I said to Uncle Eric one night over dinner. "Surely the Germans will run out of puff now they've got all of Europe. It gives our armies a chance now, to plan a strike back."

"I wish it were so, boy," he answered with a rise of his bushy eyebrows, "but what can we strike back with? We are unprepared. Where were the British Spitfires, best fighter plane in the world, so we're told, when the Stukas were attacking? Where were the Allied tanks as the *Panzers*, instead of trying to best France's feted Maginot line, simply came around it, through Belgium? The flaunted Maginot forts never fired even a shot in defending France. It was all talk, boy, and no action. I think we have too few of anything to mount a strike back. It will be a short war only if Germany and Japan win. If we are to win, it is going to be a very long war."

"Longer than the First World War?"

"I hope not. But we have many mountains to climb."

So all the big talk on the wireless, I now realised, was wishful thinking, nowt but empty propaganda, same as what Mr. Churchill said about Mr. Atlee—'all puff and no spittle.'

Mum had let me bring the Big Book. She was selling all Dad's books, so I at least salvaged the atlas. The big globe had to go. I wondered what other familiars from our house would be missing when Mum arrived back in Sydney.

Had it been only the globe and not the atlas I had for my future work, I would have had the big job of starting my map all over again with all Europe coloured a creamy sort of brown rather than green.

And how would I have traced it from a globe?

~ * ~

Uncle Eric and Aunty Grace made me welcome. They had two daughters but no son, so Mum had warned me that I shouldn't expect they'd find it easy coping with an eleven-year-old bundle of enthusiasm like me. I never quite understood what she meant by that, but I at least got the message that I shouldn't expect them to know me as well as had Dad. So I treaded things cautiously. As nearest brothers in a big family they had ever been close, and Aunt Grace was not a stroppy sort of aunt. She seemed to understand about boys, because I found her like Mum in many ways. I fitted in there pretty well.

They were happy about my interest in the war because they also followed events closely. It was them gave me my first hints about treating news reports with caution.

"Have you ever noticed, lad, how good news always reaches us in a matter of days, while bad news takes a month? We read into that, that maybe very bad news doesn't reach us at all. We simply have to be content that the authorities are doing the best they can for us. They have to keep up morale, even if only to support a faith for a better future."

That one, of course, I had to take to bed with me and really ponder on.

Uncle Eric was a master builder but now had only older men as tradesmen and labourers—and if you added increasing shortages of materials to his problems, he had to put much of his business 'on the back-burner' as he called it. So he now hired out his skills to the war effort and was building accommodation blocks and things for the army. Weekends he was dig, dig, dig under his house building an air raid shelter, and I was hired in exchange for pocket money to help him. He did things the right way, I reckoned, and I'm not talking about the art of building—I'm talking about how he enlisted my services. Before dangling the pocket money carrot in front of my nose, he spread out his very professional-looking plans of what he was building. He knew all the local inspectors at the council, of course, and it being his own house he was working on, they had illustrated their respect for him by simply rubber-stamping all the approvals he sought and simply told him to go home and get on with it.

He knew all about stresses and things, so knew exactly how much reinforcing he had to include so his entirely brick-and-tiled house couldn't collapse into the shelter... "Or even any part of it," he insisted with a laugh.

I never ceased to envy Val, however, living with Moogs and Lance. But only in one respect, and that was that Uncle Lance had fought in the First World War and been captured in Flanders. He was taken to Germany as a prisoner of war and had great tales of how he'd had to work for the German war effort—even in the snows of winter, a situation Aussies had never experienced, for it was very few Aussies who had ever seen snow. For that they received the 'luxuries,' as he termed it, of black bread and water twice a day. He seemed always careful when recounting what hadn't been 'too bloody nice' about his time as a POW, but he was still able to spin a good yarn for a kid rapt in every facet of war... "Albeit in such olden times," as I told him.

I found I had but one, not two, years to go in primary school. NSW had a different system from Queensland because education came under state government controls rather than federal, so things varied. When I moved from one to the other, I found I was backward in some subjects but streets ahead in others. So I felt sorry for kids whose fathers were transferred to a number of different states in turn, because they would have that problem every time they moved. However, Uncle Eric talked with cousin Wyn. She'd come out of retirement to go back to high school teaching so younger women teachers could join the Women's Military Corps. She was married to Ken Richardson, son of my Dad's eldest brother, who now was Uncle Harold's general manager. He was currently sitting in the boss's chair while Harold was off to England—hopefully safely.

It was worked out by all and sundry that it was best for me to go into the little that was left of my all-but-final year at Willoughby Primary School, and Val would wait and begin classes at Willoughby Girls High School, a 'worthy' North Shore school as it was termed, come the new year. Both were on the same campus and within walking distance of Uncle Eric's Northbridge home. Desolie, Eric and Grace's younger daughter, was beginning her second year there. Also, Aunt Wyn, a teacher there, could watch over both girls. Des and I could walk to school together each day, about two miles, and for Val it was only a short tram-ride in the opposite direction. Des and Val, therefore, would be seeing each other daily, albeit studying at levels a year apart. So Des became my 'adopted' sister as far as 'home' was concerned, and we hit it off pretty well. She told her parents, though in fun, that it was about time they provided her with a brother.

I thought that a pretty neat way of putting it.

~ * ~

It didn't take long for me to make friends at school, although none lived in the Northbridge direction. Most lived, by sheer coincidence, close to where I had lived before moving to Queensland. In fact we worked out that several were baptised at the same church as Val and me—where Mum and Dad married. So whilst my memory of it wasn't all that strong, for I'd been only a nipper when leaving for Queensland, there were still many landmarks I recognised.

But the war remained unkind. Nazi Germany appeared unstoppable. Having occupied all of Western Europe save the four countries that Germany saw selfish reasons to let remain neutral, it now had Russia, Italy, and Turkey along with far-off Japan in its Axis Bloc. Italy had occupied Albania and impetuously, as the Italians were beginning to illustrate was endemic in them, invaded Greece without doing enough homework. The Greeks responded with guerrilla-type warfare—hit-and-hide tactics that the Italians had no answer to. The Greeks would deliberately cede ground to the Ities then quickly close a pincer movement behind them to destroy their unprotected supply column, force the troops in the trap to surrender, and score all their armaments. The Italians were quickly driven back over the Albanian border, and the Allied world cheered.

"Ities are the sort of people who would rather be singing and going to the opera than playing at soldiering," Uncle Eric explained.

The Balkan countries of Hungary and Romania had been assisting the *Reich* but choosing to maintain an officially neutral stance, same as the United States was doing for the Allies. That left Bulgaria and the several smaller Balkan states waiting, fingers to mouths, not wanting to declare one way or another. Greece now knew exactly where it stood.

"You know, lad," Uncle said as dinner finished, "the Aussie volunteers are not far from that part of the world. They are in Egypt and Palestine, very near Greece. Go get your atlas."

So Des, her sister Betty and Aunt Grace cleared the table, and we all together pored over the map of southeast Europe and the eastern Mediterranean.

"Hitler won't accept the Italians being driven off by the Greeks," said Uncle. "My bet is that he'll either land crack German troops in Albania, or he'll right now drive *Blitzkrieg*-fashion through these helpless Balkan states and attack Greece from the north."

I laughed.

"You think you're Monty then?"

"General Montgomery to you, my boy. Let's give him the credit he deserves. But I'd like to check our opportunities of quickly getting our troops to that part of the world. If we cannot, Greece will be overrun as easily as Poland and France. Yet it's difficult when not knowing what naval strengths we have in the Mediterranean. The Turks and Russia will have Egypt's Aegean Islands covered, of course."

He let his fingers massage his chin as he pondered.

"No," I said. "I don't reckon we can get forces there in time. Hitler's proved himself a dab at *Blitzkrieg*. He seems always to have plenty of men and armoury right where he needs it. I reckon we've just got to wait and see."

What was to happen in that part of the world would only be known when the knife-edge slipped.

Wow! Was this ever a war, to have me studying geography?

I vowed then that when it came time for me to go to high school, where a kid had some choice in what subjects he wanted to take, I would choose both history and geography.

Four

It was getting towards Christmas, with me thinking more about Dad, who had always been a great one for Chrissy spirit. I tried not dwelling on him, because many grown-ups had said during the hectic rush to quit Brisbane that I must be strong about losing him when so young. And I stayed strong. Whenever I would start to feel sad that he wasn't around any more, nor ever would be, I'd force myself to think of all the kids in Europe who'd lost not only fathers, but entire families. Even homes.

So I was pretty well off, really.

Yet now I had a different problem to worry about.

Had Mum been around I could have bounced it off her, but she wasn't. So I was feeling pretty much alone. At least I'd be seeing Val at the Chatswood flicks come Saturday, because the air raid shelter was finished—and even the shopping. There had been a lot of that, of course, cans of this and cans of that, flasks of water and blankets.

"But no bottles," Uncle had said. "We don't want slivers of glass flying about."

Aunt Grace had its bunk-type beds made up ready, and it had two doors—"In case one gets blocked by falling masonry," said Uncle.

Pretty smart thinking, I reckoned.

Of friends made at school it was Laurie Browne I'd taken a fancy to; he more than any of the others was a 'me' person. Maybe it was because he lived in the very street I lived in before moving to Brisbane. I hadn't known him then but had walked past his house many times, it being between my house and the tram-stop. When I met Mrs Browne she said she should likely recognise my mother by sight. And she did when on my next visit I showed her a picture of our family taken in our Brisbane garden.

Laurie was a Boy Scout and never stopped talking about how much he enjoyed everything about it: the other boys, the leaders, the mind-games they played every week—"Real bloody teasers they are," he reckoned. He'd been on a camp in the bush—a Jamboree—Abo word for 'meeting of the tribes' or something like that. Scouts from all North Shore troops came together.

My problem was that I wanted to join but would have to buy my own uniform—far too expensive for me to save from pocket money. I didn't want to ask Uncle with his business on the back-burner and me costing a lot because Aunt Grace never stinted on food, and me always included in hand-outs of anything even though not their real son. I came down to asking Val's advice come Saturday. She had told me Moogs and Eric liked the idea of us going to the flicks same as when in Brissie while Mum and Dad were at tennis.

"It's a good way for you and Kev to keep in touch, talk about private things," she told Val.

I also liked the flicks because of the newsreel on how the war was going.

Val wasn't able to help me with money, and that wasn't a disappointment because I knew she had none anyway. It's just that I wanted to tell someone who would understand. Ego had been no bloody help.

~ * ~

On the war front, things remained hectic and bad.

Hungary, Slovakia, and Romania had joined the Axis bloc.

"Damn!" said Uncle when it came over the wireless at breakfast. "But it's not unexpected. The way the war's going, any nation would realise that to side with the Allies is only inviting Hitler to invade.

Romania, though, has been selling oil to the Nazis all along. It has huge oilfields, so now their oil will go a-hundred-bloody-percent to the Germans. Hitler will insist on that."

I'd never heard Uncle swear before, so it really showed how important he saw this latest bad news. But next morning the news was good.

Graf Spee, Germany's biggest battleship, was visiting Uruguay in South America, getting some repairs and being reprovisioned. The Allies knew she was there and waited offshore. The international agreement was that neutral countries could sell services to either side, but there was a limit as to how long a ship could stay in the safety of neutral ports. Uruguay simply told the German embassy that if the *Graf Spee* didn't leave, it would be impounded until the end of the war.

Oh, what a dilemma for her captain, knowing three Allied ships, all primed and ready, were waiting out there in the Atlantic. To be attacked from three sides at once would be fatal.

HMS Exeter was a British heavy cruiser, and the other two, *Ajax* and *Achilles*, both light cruisers of the New Zealand navy. I looked up the three names in Uncle's encyclopaedia—Exeter was a city in England, and Ajax and Achilles were names from champion warriors in Greek history.

I was so impatient that night I couldn't sleep. I crept out of bed and turned the wireless on, but there were only crackles.

Should any kid, I asked Ego, *have to live through such torture?*

Yet, come breakfast, all we got was that there was a big battle in progress.

It was the talk of the school. The long summer holidays were coming up, but the thought of it being Christmas was the farthest from kids' minds that it could be.

And the news that night was the best ever. *Graff Spee* was damaged so badly that the captain scuttled her rather than let her fall into enemy hands. The *Exeter* was badly damaged, but *Ajax* and *Achilles* got off a little lighter—or that's what we were told.

~ * ~

The week before Christmas, Mum arrived. She would stay a guest in the big house of Aunty Ida's parents-in-law.

Christmas dinner at Northbridge had Eric and Grace, Betty and Des, Moogs and Lance, Mum, Val, and me all together.

And my new family gave me two Christmas presents: a real scooter, coloured the gaudiest yellowy-orange I've ever seen—"For you to use for Aunt Grace's shopping," said Uncle with a grin.

And the other present was even better... "How would you like to join the Boy Scouts?"

Well! All I could think was that Val had told Moogs, and Moogs had telephoned Eric. And when I posed that to them after my tummy had settled enough, they affirmed that that was exactly it. I asked if I could use the telephone, and I rang Laurie with the good news. He said he would get the papers from his troop at the next meeting.

"Call me when you get them. I'll ride over to your place on my scooter."

It was only two miles.

~ * ~

After the Battle of the River Plate, a spark was back into everyone's eyes.

I was beginning to realise how much bravery there was in man, even Germans who kept firing even though their crew was being further decimated every minute. There was a lot of 'meat' in so many of the stories on the wireless, and I admired people on both sides, but of course I'd never dare put that into words either on the street or at school—I'd likely be lynched.

But after Christmas and my birthday, school started again. Des and I would walk together and chat over kid-things like what we wanted to do when grown-up. And Des had a really wild scheme.

"I'm never going to marry," she said, "I'm going to be a career woman."

Well, what was I to make of that?

"What, have a baby-clothes shop or something?" That was the only sort of business I'd ever heard of a woman running.

"No, silly. I'm going to work in business. I'm the only girl at Willoughby High in the business class. And that's what I am going to do."

Well that really gave me something to think on, because I had come to see Des as someone with a real grasp of realities in the world. But when I started to question her further on it, Ego pulled me up with a start.

Back off! he shouted. *Leave it. Just wait and see what happens.*

So I'd wait. I'd come to trust Ego.

Sometimes on our walk to school, our arrival would coincide with Val coming off her tram from the other direction. We'd chat a bit and agree to meet again at the usual time at the *Arcadia* flicks come Saturday. We wished each other good luck in joining our new classes. Val was moving into first-year high, Des into second, and me into my final year primary.

My 'Mrs. Allison' figure was a man—Mr. Wyatt, an old fellow, for all young teachers were off to war. But he seemed okay. When he realised I was newly from Queensland, he came straight out with, "Well, young man, you can help me teach the rest of these boys about this year's levels for spelling and parsing—but you'll have to do twice the homework they do in arithmetic."

Well, I thought—I reckoned I shouldn't have too much trouble coping with any of that.

Laurie was in my class, and we paired at a desk. And I liked the schoolwork. Same as in Brissie, instead of using exercise books—for there was a real paper shortage—they dug up old-fashioned slates from somewhere, and we had slates for writing on.

And I joined the Scouts—First Chatswood Troop, oldest troop in the district, for there was even an Eighth Chatswood not too far away. Many of the boys were also schoolmates, yet there were many other new friends. There were lots of interesting activities, of course, both indoor and outdoor, and even war-work, all adding up to the additional adventure I'd sought. We were co-opted into military first aid and visited army camps, learning camp-cooking alongside servicemen—even stretcher-bearing—all absolutely Magic Stuff in my book.

The troop had a fine record of awards in scouting. I saw the opportunity of contributing my bit by earning as many arm-badges as possible. Arm-badges were awarded for proficiency in a variety of activities, and I took up many such challenges. "Don't try to take on too much at once," I was warned. But I was ambitious and in a hurry. If the Japs advanced south as quickly as Germany had advanced in Europe, I wanted to be ready to do my bit. I couldn't get into the war to help turn back the tide of the enemy advance, but making a visible success of scouting seemed a good way of contributing. Fairly quickly, I passed for badges in Swimming, Life-Saving, Ambulance-Aid, Bushcraft, Oratory, Camp-Cooking, World History, Geography, and numerous other skills—not all at once, but I kept up regular study on more. But that's getting a bit ahead of things...

Just that I'm so impatient to get closer to doing something for the war effort!

Oh, how the waiting was proving tedious.

~ * ~

Aussie forces were known as Diggers, the name dubbed on them not solely because of all the trenches Aussies dug during the First World War, but also because of the gold-rush days during the prior century. Every state had had its share of 'the Diggings,' as goldfields were termed.

Our Diggers in Egypt had, during 1941's January, wrested off the Italians the town of Bardia just across the Egyptian border in Libya. The Ities had had a pretty effortless surge along the Mediterranean coast from the west, with eyes on the Suez Canal. But they were soon stopped when fronted by our Diggers. We captured not only the town, but also forty thousand prisoners.

The Germans must have been pretty upset with the Ities, because they sent in their own crack tank divisions in great numbers. They wrested Bardia back again because the Aussies were short on tanks. Then they continued east until the Diggers made a stand at El

Alamein in Egypt. German and Italian troops there had to dig in. The Aussies, however, encircled the entire town and, with the British navy patrolling the coast, held the town to siege.

"We'll starve the buggers out," the Diggers declared.

~ * ~

And we did. By April, however, as expected, Germany invaded Greece from Albania and, at the same time, Bulgaria and the Balkan states. I fairly quickly had the entire southeast of Europe coloured green on my map.

"It really doesn't matter what colour you have it in, lad," Uncle told me, "it still means that the Nazis now control every inch of the European continent except only the few neutral countries. They have certainly proved themselves 'unstoppable.'"

The entire world was obviously now in the gravest danger. And before anyone could imagine that things could get even worse, the Germans began sending wave after wave of bombers across the English Channel every night to bomb English cities—London, their favourite target. The poor bloody Pohms thought up every defence they could think of. They had not enough fighter-planes to combat the *Luftwaffe* that they could attack the bombers direct, so let giant balloons soar into British skies, tethered to earth by cables strong enough to cripple any aeroplane flying into them.

"This at least," Uncle explained, "means the bombers have to fly at such an altitude that their bombs cannot be trained on specific targets—so the bombing is more at random. They might miss the factories they are after, but more people in their houses are being killed. Let's hope the Americans can get more fighter aircraft to Britain in the short term."

What was to be named the "Battle of Britain" raged in the air for not months but the next two years—hundreds of thousands of people's homes being destroyed and hundreds of thousands of Britons being killed. As England was able to produce more fighters, the Spitfire and the Hurricane in particular, it was able to make a more even fight of things—but at a terrible cost of life in the air as well as on the ground. Many Aussie airmen were piloting British fighters by now.

Word filtered through to us that on the tenth of May, Rudolph Hess, deputy premier of Nazi Germany, flew a *Messerschmitt* fighter into Scotland.

Why?

This was the big question. The official word was that he was appealing to the British to put a stop to the terrible war. But the official word didn't go as far as to say whether or not it was expected Britain should surrender.

"Are we expected to believe that Hitler would listen to an appeal to parley?"

"Hitler didn't keep 'parley promises' even before the war," the smart ones answered.

"Was Hess running away? Was he sent as a spy?"

Oh the drama! I pored over reason after reason as I lay in bed trying to think why the second most important man in Germany would do such a thing; whether he came or was sent, the risks he ran were incredible! What did he hope to gain?

It was well known, it seemed, that he was personally fond of England, had visited many times and had many friends there—but really!

And it was a black day for Britain when the Royal Navy's flagship *HMS Hood* was sunk in the Baltic Sea. The German Battleship *Bismarck*, biggest warship in the world, had sunk it, so overnight became an especial target.

"Sink the *Bismarck*," was Churchill's simple order.

He didn't have to add 'at any cost' or anything like that, because we all knew the British Navy always followed orders without question.

Every long-range British plane was sent scouring the Atlantic Ocean until the *Bismarck* was sighted. Naval ships converged on it, attacking from all sides, and a torpedo crippled the big ship, jamming the rudder, which left her pretty-near helpless.

To me, jamming her rudder was just like Paris of Troy shooting an arrow into Achilles' heel. I'd read up on that after finding that one of the River Plate hero ships was named *Achilles*. Just then, however, a fog rolled in, and *Bismarck* slipped away. She was eventually found trying to make the safety of the Bretagne coast. She was shelled unmercifully before nearing the coast, however, until she sank.

"Britain again rules the waves," I told my family when that good news reached Australia with all speed. I slept with a smile on my face that night, despite the fact that German bombers were again, no doubt, bombing poor old London.

Five

A new chapter in life began when Mum took a flat in Crow's Nest.

Tears were shed at leaving Northbridge, but with the wider family so close, it wasn't goodbye. Val had a matching scene at Chatswood, for we had both been made feel very much at home with our 'adopted' families.

On our first night in our new home, despite all were tired from the work of moving, our all having arrived by sea-freight, Mum sat Val and me down for a serious talk. She wanted to apologise for having only a flat and not a house.

"With his particular sickness," she explained, "your dad forgot to pay an instalment on his life assurance, due the week he was in hospital. The policy lapsed."

Through tears she told us how she "...fought tooth and nail, trying to get them to realise your dad wasn't responsible during that time—but they insisted on 'the letter of the law' and refused to pay a penny. So despite the good job your dad had, we were left not very well off.."

On arriving in Sydney, she had gone with Uncle Harold, who had returned safely from England, to the insurance company's head office, but without success.

"So things won't be as easy as we had it before," she said as she gave us extra cuddles. But at least we were together again. We kids knew we could be tough, too, that we needed to help Mum as much as we could. We started by saying that with all the homework we now had in our new schools, we hadn't the time to go to the flicks any more. And for a long time, we didn't.

"Anyhow," I insisted, "with all the badges I'm training for at Scouts, and with all the first aid classes, my weekends are pretty well all taken up anyway."

It was a fact.

~ * ~

The flat wasn't small. It was the entire top floor of a 'duplex' for which Mum had to pay a rent £1.12.6 a week—a bloody fortune! But it had a downstairs entrance facing the street, the 'under-stairs' being box-room and tool-cupboard. I'd learned some carpentry skills building Uncle's air raid-shelter, and now armed with Dad's extensive array of tools, for he had been an amateur handyman, I fitted up shelves and racks that, along with the old tool-chest, made a workshop that could be closed off. Atop the stairs was an open veranda off which was a large living room with fireplace and in turn a little central hallway. Off it were two bedrooms, a bathroom, and a dining room. Off the dining room were a kitchenette and a small veranda off which, in turn, was a laundry. An outside stairs went down to a lawn and garden to share with the downstairs flat.

Mum took one bedroom, Val the other. I had the front veranda. Canvas blinds gave me privacy from the street on one wall and from neighbours in another.

The suburb of Crows Nest was a pinnacle—a five-way intersection, all roads leading downhill. Two were the grand Pacific Highway, one arm leading up from the Sydney Harbour Bridge to continue beyond the junction to the upper North Shore to become the Pacific Highway to Brisbane. Third 'spider-leg'—for from the air Crows Nest must indeed look like a great five-legged spider, its broad legs stretching in various directions—led west to harbourside suburbs, the fourth northeast to Willoughby and Chatswood, and the fifth east to Mosman and eventually Manly on the coast. It was certainly central, and public transport was good—tramlines branching off along four of the five feeder-roads. Within a block from our home, Val and I had a tram service direct to our different schools.

All in all, we were happily accommodated. Mum, too, was happy because we were but two short blocks of Aunty Ida.

The war, however, was not such a happy story.

In the Atlantic, U-boats were having what the Americans called a 'turkey shoot.' I'd never seen a turkey but knew from movies it was a bird Americans ate at Christmas. I found out some time later what a 'turkey shoot' was.

America shipped food and war supplies to England, a country nearly starving, of course, with rationing severe. Australia was shipping dairy products and wool from our vast resources, and America was shipping everything from small arms to anti-aircraft weapons, mortars, torpedoes, and tanks. American-built aircraft made their own way with Canadian pilots, through the clouds, refuelling in Nova Scotia and Iceland.

With so many vital supplies crossing the Atlantic, convoys were specific targets for the Nazis, and Germany had a huge submarine fleet. Guarded convoys were the normal course, scores of laden merchantmen at a time surrounded, as one might imagine, by naval destroyers, battleships, minesweepers, and anti-submarine vessels. German submarines needed to spend considerable time on the surface where they could run on diesel engines, conserving limited battery power for when submerged—I learned that at school. U-boats preyed on the surface by night, diving only once a victim was sighted, to attack with torpedoes. Air-surveillance was the surest way of spotting them by day, but the limits of the longest-range aircraft operating out of Britain, Ireland, Iceland, Canada, and the United States could not cover the entire Atlantic. A huge 'black hole' existed in which U-boats could maraud in safety. Every ship the Germans could sink was weakening both Britain's defensive and attacking strengths. Both Americans and Britons were desperately trying to build surveillance aircraft with greater range. Why Germany never invaded Iceland, which England held with a not too strong force, to wrest that important centre of North Atlantic airspace from the Allies, I'll never know. To me it would have given them a great advantage.

But I kept that thought a secret between Ego and me. If I were to tell even Laurie, word might just somehow seep through to Hitler, and I'd then feel really shitty.

Over Britain, German bombers targeted manufacturing centres, and in Southeast Asia, Japan's invading forces were getting closer to Australia, major supplier of food and equipment to all Allied forces south of the equator.

The age for military service was increased, and kids at school were saying how their fathers were now getting called up.

"Had your father not died, when he did," Mum said, "he would have had to leave work now, to go into the services."

She was finding it hard, cost-wise. Prices for food were rising as shortages increased, shortages because increasing quantities of our agricultural produce and canned meats were being shipped to England.

"I'm taking in a border," Mum said.

Mum and Val began sharing a bedroom, and Roy Griffiths came to live with us. He was younger than Dad would have been, but hadn't been called up because he worked in 'essential services.' He was a baker and worked with Sargent's Pies that made food for not only retail shops but for the fighting men.

"We pack tons of cooked meat in cans for the troops as well as for England," he told us. Roy was a bonzer bloke in every way. He had a good sense of humour despite working long and staggered hours, sometimes all through the night.

"The factory operates non-stop," he told me. "Three shifts of eight hours, seven days a week, and sometimes we must work two of those shifts in the same day. Machines stop only for maintenance."

But he had a deep interest in the war, and on the limited occasions we were home at the same time, and not abed, we'd swap notes. And it was about now that I started to get the feeling that I knew more about where all these countries in Europe were than he knew.

But the war continued exciting stuff. Rather than spend money on newspapers, for they were getting thinner as well as pricier, we spent increasing time at the wireless. Some stations now broadcast around the clock. The war had me in absolute thrall. I was ever confident of winning, however, even when the news was bad, because while England had its Sir Winston Churchill and we had our Sir Robert Menzies giving such stirring speeches, how could we not get swept along the same path of confidence? And they had it right on the ball, I reckoned—if everyone stuck together, we would defeat the Germans, Ities, and Japs, hands down.

I was simply so lucky to be living in such a time!

Then Germany again did the old Hitler trick of turning on friends. It really hit the headlines when Germany surprised the world by invading Russia—a sneak attack that took the Ruskies quite by surprise. In what seemed no time the *Werhmacht* pushed the Russians not only out of Poland but right back into the industrial heartlands of the Ukraine.

Back to the atlas I rushed.

"Russia? Ukraine?" It was an entirely new theatre of war for me to wallow in.

Then Britain took a leaf out of Hitler's 'how-to' manual. Just two weeks after Germany invaded Russia, British and Russian forces marched into Persia—another new front.

I'd never much worried about the Middle East. Only Arab countries I knew about were in Africa, but Persia was in Asia.

"An entirely new war, it almost seems," I said to Roy.

"Persia has oil," Roy explained. "Churchill knows that with Germany now attacking Russia, we must secure Persia's oil before the Axis gets to it. Persia's border with Russia must be protected at all cost."

At school, Mr. Wyatt thought it likely the King of Persia asked the Allies to come help him keep that oil from the Germans. Well, whether this was right or not, I wasn't to know.

But it certainly made clever sense.

~ * ~

The end of the year brought a whole new change of events, not only altering the entire twist of the war, but introducing another quarter of the world to my sphere of study: the Russian front.

Before the Germans could capture the major cities of Leningrad in the north and Stalingrad in the south, the 'impossible' Russian winter bogged them down at those cities' gates. No man or machine could move in the slush and bitterly cold conditions of a Russian winter.

I'd never realised that some parts of the world had such conditions. Few Aussies had ever seen snow, including me, so how could we really appreciate what bitterly cold weather was like? If I ever felt cold, I'd just pull on a jumper. But winter in Russia, it seemed, was like being in another world. Newspaper photos showed men rugged up with ice even forming on their noses and beards.

Wow! If anyone were to ask me what I thought about why the Germans would even want that part of the world, I simply wouldn't know what to answer. If I were a Russian, I'd be happy to give it away to anyone who'd take it. Whilst the Germans couldn't physically attack because they'd just sink to their haunches in snow, it seemed that their guns weren't completely frozen. They kept up a relentless barrage of fire during the entire winter, both cities being reduced to a shambles, with the people not already killed by gunfire dying of starvation. I reckoned they might be better off dead anyway, rather than having to live in a place like that.

Closer to the real world, the Japs had occupied the entire Indo-Chinese peninsula and invaded Malaya by sea. Many beachheads were established, and the Aussie Eighth Division was there trying to drive the marauders back into the sea. But we were outnumbered twenty to one.

One Digger was quoted as saying, "We've got a million bloody Japs in front of us and impenetrable jungle at our backs."

"A stand will be made at Singapore," I told Laurie and mates at school. "Singapore is impregnable. The wireless said so."

But I got home to hear the worst news of all for Aussies. In the Indian Ocean, just off our very coastline, our very own HMAS *Sydney* had been sunk by a German raider—the worst of it being that it went down with all hands.

Our whole country was aghast. Flagship of the Aussie navy!

Could things get worse?

They did. On the eastern front, the Germans reached Moscow, Russia's capital. But like in Leningrad, they got bogged down by slush. So they'd 'dug in'.

But things were happening thick and fast. The very next day, 8 December, we got news of yet another war-front opening. "Today," the wireless was saying, "hundreds of bombers from the Japanese fleet-air-arm, accompanied by submarines, without warning attacked Pearl Harbour to score a devastating victory against the United States. Most of the American fleet, caught at its moorings, has been destroyed. Thousands of service personnel have been killed."

Well! What could I say? The Japs had proved themselves no more trustworthy than the Germans! And the Americans had been caught with their pants down just as badly as was Europe when Hitler invaded Poland!

By now of course, I'd learned not only how come it was night-time at home when daytime in other parts of the world, but also how, whilst it was December 8 here, it was still only yesterday where this new war started. But that fact was, alone, just a 'fly-in-the-ointment' compared to America being brought into the world war after all this time.

It was an event to funnel the history of the entire world along a channel no one could have foreseen.

I was again totally swept along with the surge, living every moment of the action as I pored over my atlas. I had to index a double-page spread—the great Pacific Ocean.

The index tabs I'd pasted with flour and water to war-front pages in my atlas now numbered a score!

Six

The year 1942 was to be a big one for me.

Mum was now working, part-time housekeeper for the Smeal Family, the friends she had stayed with while house-hunting for our flat, and part-time in Mosman in the house of a widower. So with Roy paying rent, things were getting better for us.

January was the long lay-off from school at the end of every year—six weeks holiday taking in Christmas, New Year, and my birthday, before the next school year started in February. I was to start high school. I had got good grades and passed for Fort Street High, a GPS (Great Public School) on the south side, over the Harbour Bridge. However because of the war, it being realised that the Harbour Bridge would be the Japs' first target if ever their bombers were able to reach Sydney, and of course it was always possible that they could use aircraft carriers like at Pearl Harbour, schoolkids were not allowed any more to cross the harbour for school.

The old Greenwoods school at North Sydney, immediately on the north side of the harbour, co-incidentally the school my father had attended as a kid, was turned into a Tech-High—my 'alma mater.' It was but a fifteen-minute tram ride down the hill from Crows Nest.

Val had been invited to stay with Harold and Olive in their apartment at Mosman, just near the Sydney Zoo, so Mum asked me if I would like to go to Brisbane if able to get a train ticket.

"On my own?"

"There'll be conditions."

"Oh! Would I ever!"

"I've already sounded out Reecy," Mum said, "and you can stay with her."

Now Reecy was one of Mum's old Bridge Club friends from our Brisbane days—a big and buxom lady with a great disposition, a habitual, hearty laugh, and a heart of gold. She had always loved us kids, who had ever considered her 'family.'

"Well, you get on the tram and go see if you can get a train ticket. That's the hurdle that will decide if you can go or not. Trains are for troop movement now, and you're going to have to tell a lie or two, I would guess, if you're going to get a pass."

I put on my thinking cap and went to town. The central city ticket office, I knew, was in Martin Place. This was to be my first test at having to do anything like this. Business things had always been handled by family grown-ups. So here was me with my thirteenth birthday looming, already grown-up enough it seemed, charged with the responsibility of wangling my own train ticket.

They gave me a paper and told me to fill it in. There were stools and pens and an ink-well on the desk, even some spare nibs that made me wonder why someone hadn't nicked them by now. So I had to read through all the form...

Desired destination: 'Brisbane' I wrote.

Reason for needing a train pass: 'My sister is being married in Brisbane and I need to be there.'

What date do you wish to depart?: '7.1.1942'

What date do you wish to return?: '20.1.1942'

Then there were questions about my name, address, age, and seemingly lots of things that I didn't feel should be any of their business, but I answered them because I needed the ticket. The old man at the counter, when I handed in the form, not too smudged, I thought, despite I'd made a bit of a mess trying to write a flourishing signature, reached for a rubber stamp and signed a paper that I reckoned must have been an approval.

"Take this to the ticket window. You may not be able to get a ticket for this date, although somewhere near it."

"That's all right," I told him. And at the ticket window I was asked my age.

"Twelve," I told him. Twelve got me a half-fare ticket. I showed him my school tram pass that said I was twelve, it having been issued last year, of course. He trusted me, it seemed, for he smiled as he stamped the approval.

"Half-fare tickets don't ensure you a seat these days, lad, only your compartment. If all seats are taken, you must sit on the floor."

I nodded. That would be no hardship. It was only an overnight.

"You will have to get your return date approved in Brisbane, two days before departure," he told me.

I raced home to show my ticket, my birthday present from her, to Mum.

~ * ~

Oh the excitement of packing!

With the ticket had come an official-looking document with small print, which Mum read.

"Because of the war, civilians, and that's you, are allowed only one port. And there is a restriction on size. Go fetch my dressmaking tape."

I brought it, and we found that everything I wanted to take would have to fit in my schoolbag. I smiled at Mum's use of the word 'port' in respect of my bag. We had discovered when moving to Queensland that in that state suitcases were called 'ports,' short for 'portmanteau.' School-ports in Queensland, however, must be backpacks; "healthier for a child's spine," they insisted. On returning to school in NSW, I had been ragged unmercifully when turning up at school with my Qld regulation 'backpack.'

So my schoolbag, now a small-sized 'suitcase,' would be my only luggage except the sandwiches and fruit that Mum insisted I take. She had read on the document that because of the war, there was now no food available on the train.

"But they'll have drinking water," she said.

Mum came with me to the station.

"Hopefully there will be a lady in your compartment who can keep an eye on you."

"I'm not a child, Mum. I can look after myself."

"If I thought you couldn't, you would not be going. I simply want to be able to introduce you to someone before your start, so that at least you have some one person rather than all strangers about you if you need to ask help in any way. Now you remember about trains that there is a toilet in each carriage? You remember that..."

And so the one-sided conversation went until we arrived. I was indeed glad when we got there, because Mum's organised brain had just so many things she needed to tell me or remind me of. But finally we got there.

Every seat in my compartment was taken by service personnel— all soldiers except for two women in Air Force uniform. Only recently had the WAAFs, the Women's Auxiliary Air Force, been established. I remembered it from making the entry in my war scrapbook.

Mum clasped her hands at the sight of them. "Oh!" she exclaimed. "It's Ada and Elsie, isn't it?"

They smiled and nodded.

"Yes," they said in unison, as if practised, then laughed.

"I saw your concert in Brisbane last year," Mum said.

"We are on our way to entertain troops in the north," Mum was told.

I knew of Ada and Elsie. They were a comedy team on the wireless. We had often listened to them. And I was placed in their charge.

They seemed even excited at the prospect and assured Mum they would 'keep an eye' on me.

"Wyn Reece, an aunt, will meet him off the train," Mum said. "She will be waiting at the ticket barrier at South Brisbane Station."

I didn't know which was Ada and which Elsie, but one assured Mum that I would be 'delivered in good order.'

My tummy was turning over with excitement. And it wasn't all the excitement of the journey coming up, for I'd made this trip before with the whole family, but it was already obvious from the crowds on the platform as well as on the train that the large majority of people were in uniform of one kind or another.

I couldn't help but feel I was being invited into the very war!

~ * ~

It was hot in Brisbane.

The train ride was not comfortable but eminently enjoyable. In fact it was exciting, partly because for the first time in my life I was doing something on my very own—and with parental consent! I felt quite grown and responsible.

Ada and Elsie performed their tasks well even if not obviously so. They made it clear early in the trip that they weren't waiting until reaching 'the north' to begin entertaining the troops; they began before the fifteen-hour journey had barely started. They had every soul in our compartment, along with as many in the corridor blocking our doorway to join the fun, doubling up in laughter. Even I could cotton on to the irony in some of their jokes. It all seemed to come so naturally to them.

There were eleven people in our compartment, in the same space that used to hold eight. What had been four seats facing four others were now five and five plus me. Ada and Elsie took it on themselves to have each side take turns in squeezing up to make room for me, and the men didn't seem to mind at all. Fortunately none were fat, and I was only a skinny one. When it came time for sleeping, coins would be tossed to see who, among the adults, got to stretch out on a seat to sleep, with a third on the floor. Most of the blokes reckoned Ada and Elsie should be the two to sleep on the seats, but they insisted on being simply more uniformed personnel. The rest, including me, had to fight for space enough to sleep on the floor in the corridor or washroom. It didn't make things half difficult getting to the toilets.

And every other carriage will be the same, Ego told me.

But I didn't mind. It was the war, and I so envied all these men going to take part in it. Every one of them, I knew, had to be very brave. But all seemed in a happy enough mood on this journey.

Reecy was there to meet me. Mum had sent her a telegram to say I had got away on time.

"And when we get home, Kev," she told me, "I will phone through a telegram to her to say you arrived safe and well."

Reecy was a happy soul. I knew her shop, of course. It was not simply a 'corner store' like Mrs. Gee's; Reecy's shop was on a three-street corner. It was a general store-come-residence and had a big backyard with her own chicken-run. She also had a big aviary of parrots, many of which Mr. Reece, her husband Edgar, had taught to talk. One lived not only in the house but in the shop. Its name was Tojo—the name of the Japanese war minister. If a customer came in, Tojo would fly through the house screeching "Shop! Shop!"

Edgar wasn't allowed in the shop—except he had to mind it, for instance, when Reecy came to meet my train. But he didn't get a key to the till. Reecy had left him a reasonable amount of change loose under the counter. In the normal course, Reecy ruled her shop, including poor Edgar, like my mum ruled our house.

"Edgar steals the profits," she told me at the breakfast table, right in front of poor Edgar, who always sat quietly while Reecy talked. And she seldom stopped.

"And he sells things to his old crony mates without collecting coupons," she added. "But now you're here, Kev, you can help me in the shop. But if I have to slip out at any time, or on the phone or something, and you have the shop to yourself, you've got to promise me you won't let Edgar have the key to the till." And all this again right in front of poor Edgar as she showed me the key to the till drawer on the end of a chain around her big waist.

Poor Edgar. He was a nice old bloke, but always terribly quiet when Reecy was around. When she was busy in the shop, though, he'd have me help him feed the birds, collect hen-eggs, and do this and that, and keep up a chatter all the time. I couldn't help but feel that he was happy to have me around. Anybody around, in fact. He had a bed on a veranda, and Reecy had her own room that she kept locked day and night.

But she loved everybody else as they seemed to love her. And she was happy enough. It seemed poor Edgar lived his life with enough worries for both.

It was not too long a walk up the hill to the tram, so I would go into the city for the flicks. It was a pity it was school holiday time, though, for I'd have liked to say hello to Mrs. Allison. I took a bus to Wilston, however, to visit my mates.

And I learned where everything in the shop was shelved so I could help out with serving. Prices of everything were marked for Edgar's benefit when filling in emergencies, I reckoned, on the edge of the appropriate shelf. And all goods that needed coupons were in a special place behind chicken-wire and lock and key, with a government document pasted by it, listing how many of what sort of coupons for each product. Coupons had to be kept in the till-drawer, too.

When it came to slicing ham or something as difficult, I had to call Reecy from whatever chore she was about. But even without giving me any lecture on being honest or such, she gave me a key to the till drawer and left it up to me to take money and give out change. So that was a nice feeling, despite I reckoned she was a good enough money manager to know how much should be in the till when she reckoned up come closing time each night.

I enjoyed my holiday so much that I kept enough out of the extra pocket money Mum had given me to buy a pair of ruby earrings for her by way of thanks.

I reckoned they likely weren't real rubies, but Mum mightn't notice such a detail.

~ * ~

North-Tech was a great school.

No permanent class teacher any more, it was special teachers for special subjects. And no fixed classrooms. It was pack up and move when the alarm-clock on the master's desk went off. We didn't have teachers any more, either. We had masters and mistresses.

I chose English, Maths-1, Maths-2, History, Geography, French, and Tech Drawing as my subjects. English and Maths-1 (Arithmetic and Algebra) because they were compulsory, Maths-2 (Geometry and Trigonometry) because I was going to become the world's best architect, History and Geography because they were such exciting subjects, French because we had to choose a foreign language and who in their right mind would dare want to speak German or Japanese, and Tech Drawing—a compulsory subject if wanting to graduate into the School of Architecture at Sydney Uni. And I did. Every kid also had to select any of the 'Arts' subjects so I chose Music because when living in Brisbane I had learned to play piano. At school, though, we didn't get near a piano in music class, which was only once a week, but were taught about rhythm and metre and famous composers. And of course we had to make a choice of what sports we would play. Every kid, even sissies, had to take a winter and summer sport. I chose wisely—rugby and swimming.

Why 'wisely' you might ask?

Well, maybe that should be 'luckily' because North-Tech, while I was there, had the best rugger team of all Sydney schools. We won the trophy four of the five years I was there. I was never in the top team, of course, for it was only final-year kids that played in the GPS competition, and the year I was in fifth year I was too busy swatting. But I learned to love rugby. And swimming became part of my life— more on that later.

Most masters and mistresses were old. During the war, of course, whatever a kid wanted to do, it was always old people running it. Sometimes it wasn't bad, but at others it was terrible. A prime example was Old Crusty. He took first- and second-year students for Maths-1 and had grown up under Queen Victoria's stern gaze, we reckoned. He had that cold, hard stare as if his face were cast in concrete—like it would simply shatter into a thousand pieces if someone took to it with a twenty-pound hammer. There were many of us who would have happily swung one at him if given the chance. And he was sickly-looking as well, his entire complexion the colour of yellowing teeth.

He was just so old-fashioned as to believe kids should be seen and not heard during lessons that even when he asked a question we had to write down our answer then pass our slate to someone else, and they had to mark right or wrong. Wow! What a terrible way to teach. But we taught him a lesson or two before our first year was out…

First, we ganged up, such that every slate we got, no matter from whom, and no matter whether the answer was right or wrong, every kid put his hand up when the 'rights' were called for, then again when the 'wrongs' were called for. That soon put him in his bloody place, we reckoned.

Second, he was called Old Crusty because he was old and crusty—just the slightest hint of a halo of hair between the ears, not too far above the neckline. When it was raining, knowing that each Tuesday he'd be coming from a different building, hugging the wall so he wouldn't get too wet, we'd all crowd the windows in our third-floor classroom. We would hold the swing windows level until each pane filled with water, and having calculated how many seconds it should take for the water to drench him, we'd let the rope slip! Oh, how was this for an algebraic exercise to make Old Crusty proud of us? Getting the answer correct was hitting the target!

Even Generals Montgomery and MacArthur would have been proud of that, I'd reckoned.

When Crusty arrived in the classroom that day, every kid sat with angelic smiles; inside of course, hearts were thumping.

It was at North-Tech that I acquired the nickname Ric. All kids had their name shortened of course, it was an Australian trait, and Richardson was far too long a name to be serviceable. Of my best mates Laurie Browne became 'Brownie,' Bryan Lyne 'Lynie,' and Ken Midson, who was fatter than Boswell back at Windsor State, became 'Middy.' We were to remain a staunch foursome for all our five years there.

~ * ~

When the 'impregnable' Singapore fell to Jap forces, the entire division of Aussie servicemen defending Australia was captured along with British and Indian troops. Every gun emplacement on the island faced seawards: east, south, and west. The only approach to Singapore was by sea. The 'impossible' jungles of the Malay peninsular in the north were so thick that there was no road—there was not even a northern possibility to defend. Yet that was the way the Japs came, undetected and in force. They had sliced pathways through the jungle with machetes and made tracks wide enough for pushbikes! Yes, bicycles! Singapore, would you believe, was taken by pedal-power!

"How sneaky," all my mates agreed! Australia's entire Eighth Division found themselves prisoners of war before they could even fire a shot. And all the British residents, shopkeepers, and administrators, and the most state-of-the-art shipyards in the entire East, were just served up to the Japs like a tasty breakfast waffle.

My mind, when hearing of so many of our boys being captured and in Changi Prison, flew to Uncle Lance when a POW in the First World War, living on nothing but black bread and water.

"But Japanese don't eat bread," we were told at school. "They eat only rice and fish."

People began writing to the newspapers suggesting we should negotiate with the Japanese that we could send food parcels to our Diggers, foods they found palatable. But the government said we could never trust the Japanese, that they were the world's greatest liars, that anything we sent would be given to their own troops. Wow—what a situation!

But what the authorities now realised was that with no Singapore— no 'last line of defence'—there was now no barrier to a Japanese invasion of Australia. Like the Germans in Europe, Japan had raced through Indo China, were charging west into Burma, and had hardly had to slow down in their race through the 'impenetrable' jungles of Malaya that lay to their south.

It was never in the newspapers of course, nor given out over the radio, but word of mouth spread across the country that a road was being 'frantically' built north to Darwin, that troops and heavy equipment could be sent there. There'd never before needed to be a road to Darwin, because it could be easily reached by sea. Now, however, the superior Japanese Navy made trying to ship into Darwin too risky.

Barbed wire fences were being installed along the entire north coast to hinder any full-scale landing.

"But we have no army to defend the defences! They're all in Changi prison!"

What a helpless realisation!

Winston Churchill was again asked to release the Aussie forces in the north of Africa and the Middle East. But the hard answer was "No!" Defending the Suez Canal and driving the Germans out of Africa was vital to the global war effort.

"More important than saving Australia from the Japanese?"

It seemed so.

Yet even I could see that bringing our forces from that part of the world would be like a drop of water in the ocean when viewed in relation to Japan's millions of men under arms.

Australia was to be sacrificed.

America, however, with forces many times more numerous than even Britain, was aware of several criteria affecting Australia. Firstly, it had facilities to more quickly build naval strengths than had Britain's decimated industrial facilities. Secondly, if the Japanese were to occupy Australia, it then had limitless opportunities to feed its millions both at home and in theatres of war, not to mention limitless iron ore and steelworks to strengthen its armouries and naval fleets. If the United States were to defeat Japan in the long term, it was imperative that Australian natural resources be protected. Also, if the United States were to defeat Japan, it must have shipping ports and airports closer to the South Pacific area of war than Pearl Harbour. And Australia had these in abundance.

Suddenly Australia became, by virtue of necessity to the United States, vital.

A realisation I was easily able to recognise, of course.

"Even Queenslanders could likely see that," the jokesters would say!

But, even if only by default, it was to prove Australia's saving grace.

Seven

Many afternoons after school, I would tram it across the bridge to visit Sydney's largest technical library. It was housed, for the want of somewhere better, in the stately old and historic Queen Victoria Building in which one couldn't escape the stink of beer brewing in its cellar.

"How astute of the authorities to house it underground," Mum reckoned with a touch of scorn. "It's more than a little reassuring that our bureaucrats have some priorities right in such a time as this."

She was an especially happier lady these days because she'd bought herself a washing machine. It was a big round tub on legs with a gas-ring underneath so it could heat its own water—and on top was a ringer that you could wind by a handle.

Wow—what will people think of next?

But the hard fact of being at war was never brought closer to home than when the wireless reported that the Japs had bombed Darwin—actually dropped bombs on our country. I straightway made a commitment to Ego that for my family's protection I would make them an air raid shelter. Nothing as elaborate as Uncle Eric's, of course, for that was beyond me and was too costly, but big enough and safe enough for the three of us, Roy, should he be home, and Mrs. Rowling and her little son John in the downstairs flat. Mr. Rowling was off in the navy, some sort of officer on HMAS *Hobart*. Inclusion of the last three, prompted by Ego, was my contribution to community service that the government insisted every soul should consider at every moment. So with Mum's and Mrs. Rowling's approval I started digging. Oh my! What a challenge.

Brownie, my mate Laurie, was building one also, so of course mine had to be just that little bit bigger, even if only by six inches. We gave each other support, for we would daily offer encouragement, even if just to find out whose was progressing fastest. I certainly didn't want Laurie surprising me by telling me he was finished when I still had no roof on mine, for instance; so neither could quit, no matter how hard the work, without letting the other claim one-upmanship.

I had my time more than pretty well occupied, not only with school and the library and Scouts, but with the flicks. Mum wouldn't let Valerie go to the flicks alone, and her current craze in men was Nelson Eddy, a flick hero; *the Sesqui*, our local flicks, was running an every Saturday marathon of *Naughty Marietta*-type movies. Ego insisted I illustrate family support by going with her. And homework was twice what I ever had at primary school—"and considerably more important," Mum kept insisting. So my dugout was a narrow trench wide enough for a wooden bench to seat six. It had to be deep enough so the tallest of us, and that was Mum, could sit without her head bumping on the roof. It was spanned by sheets of corrugated iron that the government gave people for the purpose, with four-by-two hardwood rafters every two-feet-six apart, so the roof wouldn't sag, even with considerable rubble piled atop. The most fiddly part was the steps going down. They couldn't be wooden; they could only be earth with wooden treads. There was no sophisticated larder like at Northbridge, merely four empty jam-tins with a candle in each and a box of matches.

Over the next several months, Darwin was bombed again and again until I reckoned there could be damned-all left. They'd never tell us that part, of course, but I'd seen Movie-tone pictures of what bombing was doing to London. One kid from a Darwin family started coming to our school. All civilians, most of whom had never been 'south' in their lives, had been evacuated.

"How'd you come when there is no road," I asked. "By ship?"

"There is a road now. The army built one… well, a sort of one."

Well. The wireless had never told us that either—in case someone mentioned it to the Japanese, I reckoned. And that was easy to understand. But it really brought the war home to all the rest of us.

In the cities, everybody had to do air raid drills, and at school special concrete shelters were built in the playgrounds. Moogs and Lance, my aunt and uncle where Val had lived, with no children of their own, had two young teen-age girls evacuated all the way from England now living with them. They had 'adopted' them for the duration. Many English kids had been sent from home to escape the incessant bombings going on there.

By Easter, Japan had possession of Burma, Malaya, the Philippines, the Dutch East Indies, and Singapore. So much was happening in my life that I was beginning to find it hard to keep up with everything. A fillip came our way, however, in what we were later told was the greatest naval battle in Pacific history between Japanese, US, and Aussie navies in the Coral Sea off the Queensland coast. During it, HMAS *Hobart* was mistaken by American B17s for Japanese, and they bombed it unmercifully. Many Aussie lives were lost. The two-day battle was decisive in the outcome of the war, these later reports said, because the Japs lost two aircraft carriers.

The significant biggest 'hidden' outcome of the Battle of the Coral Sea as it was called, according to the wireless at the time, was that it was the first battle the Japanese hadn't won. It had been trying to take Port Moresby, capital of New Guinea, but failed. The United States had recently broken the Japanese Naval Code so knew where to find the fleet—a significant breakthrough to weaken the entire future of Japan's supremacy at sea, what with the Yanks having lost all their battleships at Pearl Harbour. It was also the first setback in Japan's drive south through South Pacific Islands. The loss of Japanese carriers greatly influenced the US victory at Midway in the North Pacific just a few months later.

US General Douglas MacArthur was, about this time, created supreme commander of the South Pacific War. We knew his HQ was "somewhere north of Sydney," but in later years I discovered it was a hotel on the coastline of the quiet little fishing village of Nelson Bay, north of Newcastle. When Kit and I married in 1951, we spent our honeymoon at the then Shoal Bay Country Club Hotel, only to discover that the hotel's large table where we sat for every meal had been General MacArthur's desk. On it he had spread his maps to chart the war, including the re-taking of the Philippines.

The entire headland at the bay's entrance was honeycombed with underground passages, and the entrance as fortified with cannons as had been the entrance to Sydney Harbour.

~ * ~

Right after the Battle of the Coral Sea, I was actually in the war!

Well, near enough that shells and torpedoes were exploding within earshot and eyesight. Explosions were loud enough to drown out even the air raid sirens blaring into our eardrums. Sydney was indeed under attack. Yet not from bombers.

Mum had a boyfriend.

Lou Somers was the widower living alone for whom Mum had been housekeeper a couple of days a week. The big house was right on the inner Sydney Harbour beach of Sirius Cove—so much 'right on' the beach that you walked out of his living room's French doors straight into sand. It was the last house of many built for harbour views, down a long flight of steps from Mosman's Musgrave Street West.

Sirius Cove is on the harbour's North Shore, directly opposite the Garden Island Naval base. I was sound asleep on a glassed-in veranda that overlooked the harbour while Mum slept with Lou deep in the house, where I'd been warned not to explore.

Air raid sirens suddenly blared through the still night—doubly loud, they seemed, than any drill alerts ever heard, so all the house was awake. Mum and Lou arrived on to the veranda in dressing gowns as searchlights galore, ten or twelve, of them began sweeping the harbour surface. First report to reach my ears was a great *boom!* from far off. What was happening was that three Japanese midget submarines, each carrying two men and two torpedoes, sneaked through the shipping boom built across the mouth of the main harbour; they sneaked through in the wake of a visiting ship for which the boom had been opened. The third sub got itself tangled in the net as the boom closed and couldn't free itself. Its presence became known when it was realised the boom hadn't properly closed and an investigating team of divers discovered the sub. When its occupants realised they were found, they blew themselves up, torpedoes and all. Meanwhile down-harbour where the heavy cruiser USS *Chicago* was moored, ratings on watch saw a torpedo miss it by 'inches,' they later claimed, to explode when hitting a moored ferryboat, the *Kuttabul*, a barracks for Aussie Navy personnel. Twenty died.

All this was directly opposite our windows. It was like being in the flicks and sitting in the front row!

The flash from that torpedo explosion nearly blinded me! And its 'boom' seemed to echo and re-echo through my very ears. Wow—had the war ever come close!

Now, of course, all the defence people knew there was at least one more sub in the raiding party. But how many more?

Searchlights played right into our veranda, blinding the three of us—and flares were being fired skywards, lighting up the entire scene. I've never seen my Mum looking so scared. Not only were all the naval base guns brought into play, but depth charges began exploding—not just a few, but dozens! Just a few hundred yards from us!

So the searchlights and flares had obviously picked out something.

Other torpedoes hit the dockyard wharves and exploded. Many naval ships were in port, yet none were hit—mainly because, the wireless told us next morning, the searchlights found one sub, and helicopters also with searchlights followed it into Taylor Bay, where it tried to hide. It was despatched by an absolute barrage of depth charges. We found out a week later that the sub, disabled by depth charges in Taylor Bay, the very next bay from where we were, had been raised. Its occupants had suicided.

Oh what a lovely war this is!

What a great and exciting cocktail for a lad with an adventurous heart to take to bed with him every night for the next several weeks, to colour his dreams!

The third sub had been sighted by searchlights when it surfaced for a matter of a minute or two, maybe to get its bearings, but it submerged again before more shots could be fired. It was thought that it had either been hit by depth charges in the deep centre of the harbour or blown itself up underwater. North Shore residents were warned, however, to keep a lookout should either of the personnel aboard have made it ashore.

Meanwhile, in an action to illustrate just how global was this war, the British navy attacked Madagascar, wresting the entire island off the Vichy French. I rushed to my atlas again. This was the most southerly nation in the world to sight action. And this gave Britain a base close enough to attack the Vichy French possessions of Mauritius and the Seychelles.

"It's from there the German raider that sank the *Sydney* would have been operating," I informed Mum.

We had a telephone at the flat now—a facility as hard to come by as hen's teeth. If a subscriber already had a telephone installed and was moving house, the telephone company would move the connection for you, but to have a new line connected was impossible.

"Ask again after the war," was the jocular response to any such request.

The father of one of my friends had gone off to war, and his mother, expecting air raids to start any time, was quitting their rented house to move in with a sister or something like that. So there was a spare phone to be had. My friend's mum told the telephone company she was moving into our flat and wanted the phone transferred—so we got a telephone!

And it was the very day after hearing the news about Madagascar that, when I arrived home from school, Mum said one of the people she phoned to say we now had the phone was an aunt, a real aunt this time, in Newcastle. And Aunt asked if I could come visit for the King's

Birthday weekend. There was no school for four days, and although I'd miss a Scout meeting, I wanted to go. My dad had been born in Newcastle, so I wanted to see where he grew up when little. He was the youngest child, and both his mother and father died by the time he was eight, so all the family except one brother moved to Sydney where more work was available for the older ones. All those siblings shared a house in North Sydney, where young Vic could go to school. It was the family of the brother who stayed in Newcastle that now invited me. My cousin John was as interested in the war as me. We had been corresponding quite a while. I went by train—had another sister getting married!

It was only a journey of about three hours, but the war followed me!

What was discovered in Japanese naval records after war was that the four 'parent' subs of the mini-subs that attacked Sydney waited offshore for several days for the 'minis' to rendezvous for a 'piggyback' home. One of the four 'minis' had run aground even trying to get into the harbour, and I've already told what I knew of the others. When they failed to rendezvous with the mother ships after the appointed time, it was assumed they had, if not been captured, blown themselves up. The four parent subs then, over a couple of nights, shelled both Sydney and Newcastle, expending whatever ammunition they had. Apart from such attack being of 'morale-busting' significance on the enemy, Sydney and Newcastle being the two most populated cities in that part of the country were also the most highly industrialised. So shelled they were.

So I had my second experience of being in a real, live firing line.

We could tell we were being shelled from offshore, all right. We were listening to the wireless, and it was giving us a burst-by-burst account. It was thought at first they might have been trying to shell the country's biggest steel works in Newcastle, but it was generally presumed later that they were just aiming for the shapes of the buildings standing out in the moonlight.

We didn't get hit, but for the second time in a week, I was where the action was!

~ * ~

Rationing was really starting to bite into the meals Mum could make. Eggs were rationed, but some neighbours had chicken runs, and we were able to get eggs that way. But meat was the problem. We'd always had lamb chops or beefsteaks grilled every day of the week except Sunday, when it was a huge leg or shoulder roast. Now we had to be satisfied with sausages made of what Mum reckoned were scraps and fat. Coupons for beef didn't go far at all. Maybe only once a week now were we able to have things like that.

"Makes it difficult giving you the right foods to keep kids healthy," Mum would say. But she'd always follow that up with agreeing that we had to make sacrifices. Yet she would try keeping her own spirits up, singing along with the wireless—Gracie Fields with "Wish me Luck as You Wave Me Goodbye," Vera Lynn's tear-jerkers "I'll be Seeing You" and "We'll Meet Again," and my best of all old favourites, "Shuffle off to Buffalo."

We could save on coupons, but purely by luck because of one old codger's stroke of happy aforethought. He was all wrinkled and had a beard "more bushy than the rump of a black sheep," Roy reckoned and had hit on a great idea...

Rabbits galore inhabited Australia, multi-millions of them, and farmers were tearing their hair out in lumps because rabbits ate everything green, including the crops they grew, and everything any other colour once fields were bereft of green.

The government was even paying men to go round shooting the pesky rabbits. 'Twenty-two' shot was made available for the purpose, despite the war.

Well, to me, rabbits were great tucker. I'd always loved the taste, and suddenly, along our street and every other street in Crow's Nest, this old codger would trundle his big wooden-wheeled barrow with not only skinned rabbits, in sacks to keep the flies off, but gum-tree saplings trimmed as clothes-props.

"Clothes-props a zac (sixpence), rabbits a tray (threepence)," he'd call. Women and kids would be out like a shot to buy one or the other.

We bought rabbit whenever we could because it was meat 'without coupons,' and the way Mum baked them they tasted better than fillet-steak.

"Don't you dare tell the kids at school that I serve rabbit up to you," she would make Val and me promise.

"Why not?" asked I. To grasp every opportunity of serving up baked or stewed rabbit was a treat with no equal, in my mind—unless it be Vegemite, which I insisted on having every morning of my life.

"Because it's cheap fare," Mum would reply.

In the bush, of course, farmer's wives were serving up rabbits as quickly as the farmhand could skin them. It not only helped keep down the rabbit population, but it was free. So it was difficult to fathom, sometimes, I tossed over with Ego, how some grown-ups could find things wrong when talking of even the greatest taste sensation in the world.

And then came another treat. Mum followed up the luxury of having a washing machine by adding another household innovation: She bought a fridge. She sold the old ice-chest to a neighbour, and our refrigerator worked off kerosene. How they got the idea of using heat to keep things cold I hadn't the foggiest—but that's how it was. There was plenty more space now to keep bottles of fizz-drinks and things—"Even more rabbits," I told her.

When the old codger called, from now on, I felt we should always buy two.

"To cook two at once is no more difficult than cooking one," I reasoned, "and the leftovers can be kept in the fridge for the next dinner."

But she scored a point again. "That's the only reason I bought the fridge," she told me with a laugh.

She was still as fussy with her housekeeping. We kids had learned to get by with it, and even Roy had learned to roll his eyes at us kids if he got the chance of doing it without Mum spotting it. He too had realised that she had eyes like a hawk.

"Even see around corners," he would whisper to me with a wink.

One day he pulled me aside after such an instance and said, "Why don't you ask your mum if she's written to the Queen yet, to tell her of your new address?"

So I did, just to see what she would say.

And she didn't bat an eyelid but came straight back with, "Of course. You don't think I would have forgotten something like that, do you?"

Eight

Great Uncle Fred Woolley gave me his old pushbike. He was moving to Melbourne to live with his sister Mabel, whom I'd never met. He'd been living with his sister, my gran—Mum's mum that is.

My own bike! 'Time-worn,' Uncle called it, which was really paying it a compliment.

"You can have it if you promise to go shopping for your gran once a week. She can't manage that hill on her own, and up until now I've been doing the shopping for her."

I readily agreed, for two reasons. One was that I wanted the bike. The other was that Mum was standing right by me. My gran had a bad hip, wore a high boot on one leg that wasn't high enough because it was heavy enough as it was; with a stick, she walked with a decided limp—and had to be careful on rickety footpaths. She lived not too far away, so it wouldn't be a problem for me. But I resolved to smarten-up the bike. It needed some rust spots sanded down and repainting here and there. In fact it had more places needed repainting than not. Its wheels were true, and the big chain sprocket had all its teeth—I whispered to Mum that that was more than could be said for Uncle. But she didn't rouse; she only frowned. But it was all right, because many of my mates were riding around on a lot worse. You couldn't get parts.

"Why don't they give us coupons for bike parts rather than stop making any at all?" we'd ask each other at school. Not only had bike shops run out of parts, most had closed down anyway because bikes weren't being made until after the war.

The bloody Japanese knew where to find them, when attacking Singapore, I told Ego.

"And if we don't win the war, maybe never," one of the kids at school said. He got beaten up that afternoon. Other kids waited for him when classes finished and dragged him behind the air raid shelters and made him sorry indeed for having said something so unpatriotic.

"Now I won't have to pay tram fares to school every day, or to Scouts, or to football, or the pool," I told Mum.

"Well," she answered, "now you won't need so much pocket money. I'll tell you what I reckon is fair..."

Oh-oh! Every time Mum says that I end up worse off in things...

"Now you can run messages for shopkeepers after school of a day. Mr. Gould at the greengrocers asked only the other day if I knew of a lad who could deliver for him on Friday afternoons and Saturday mornings. It'll only be for people who can't carry heavy things home. Like Gran. It's time you started to earn something towards your keep, you know."

"What does Val earn? She doesn't run messages for anyone."

"Valerie does housework after school and gets things ready for our dinner. I have to go to work to pay our rent and feed and clothe you kids."

So even money's getting rationed in our house now!

Mum always seemed to win when it came down to sharing. She had this knack of being quick with plausible answers—a fortunate knack for her and unfortunate for me. It was only later that I would think of things I could have said, yet she seemed to have thoughts ready, as if waiting on the tip of her tongue. A real gift that was. Every time she had me feeling like being pressed into a corner. I always had to give in, surrender like the Aussies in Singapore.

I sucked in a breath. "All right, Mum. I'll go round and see Mr. Gould."

"Then go to see your Gran and ask her what day she wants you to shop for her. She told Uncle Fred she'd pay you something, but you shouldn't take anything. She lives on a pension. So how about if I still pay you your usual pocket money, despite you won't have fares, and you give me two-and-six out of the four shillings Mr. Gould pays? That way you end up with enough to keep your bike on the road and also save towards your camping trips and things."

Which I thought was pretty reasonable.

But it's the way Mum goes about things, I pleaded to Ego. *She always makes everything sound so much like sharing, that a kid's got nowt to argue against.*

All us kids found the times tough. Most mates had fathers called up for the war, and Diggers didn't get anywhere near the pay that peacetime jobs paid. All mothers were stretched for pennies. I knew Mum had to work long hours for her pay. I had to buy a lamp for the bike anyway. Old Mr. Earl up the street was on to all the kids with bikes. He'd been appointed street warden, and he strutted about giving orders as if he had general's pips on his shoulders.

"You gotta have lamps on your bikes, boys. And they gotta have masks on 'em." Masks were louvres to direct light down on to the road—not to show lights that aircraft could see. Motor vehicles had louvres on their lights, too.

I bought a second-hand light with mask for two-and-ninepence. Mr. Somers, still Mum's boyfriend, a builder he was, gave me the shallow remains of a tin of black paint. I even saved money on a paintbrush. I painted the whole bike, as well as the lamp and mask, with an old toothbrush.

~ * ~

Have you ever felt you wanted to do something simply because it seemed impetuous? I often felt like it—sort of had itchy feet to be doing anything except following the boring paths of routine. It's strange because no one could say I was bored. In fact I always seemed to have things happening in my life; yet they were the same things over and over. I felt like doing something rash, something adventurous.

Tomorrow was school holiday, a Monday public holiday. And it came to me overnight. *To celebrate having my bike, I'll ride it to bloody Manly for a surf!*

Ego reckoned Manly was too far. Sure, I knew it was a long way, I'd been there once when a kid. It had a long beach with lots of surf, and in the present moment, that really appealed. I couldn't get lost because I knew it had a tramline all the way except across the Spit Bridge, where you had to leave this tram to walk across and catch another—still on the same ticket, of course. There was only one branch tramline, and that was off to Mosman and Uncle Harold's place, and I knew that junction. There was no danger of me taking a wrong turn there. I pulled on my woollen swim-trunks, then shorts, sandshoes, and a light cotton shirt. I didn't want anything that would make me sweat. I wouldn't need a beach-towel—I'd drive so fast the wind would dry me.

It was all pretty flat as far as Spit Junction, where the tramline branched off to Mosman, and I was feeling perky. I'd remembered there were some pretty steep hills getting across Middle Harbour. First was the steep, winding road down to the Spit Bridge. It had some glorious views, but I hadn't thought there would be so many bends, each leading to more steep falls. I half coasted down. Ego started hinting about the climb coming home, but I didn't want to know. I told him I'd be feeling so refreshed after my swim that the hill would be no problem. I kept thinking I was now pretty close to Manly. *It's not far the other side of The Spit*, I told Ego.

After I'd ridden across the bridge, sniggering inside at all the people off the trams having to walk across when I could ride, I had a shock. I knew Manly was about fifteen miles from Crow's Nest and was pretty sure I must have pedalled some ten or twelve by now. But on the Manly side of the bridge, at the bottom of what was to turn out to be a hill as long and steep as the one I'd just come down, was a milestone.

M8, it read. I could hear Ego whispering, *I told you so*, but I switched him off.

Before even halfway up the hill, I got off and walked the bike the rest of the way. All the people I'd seen walking across the bridge now passed by in the tram, all looking pretty bloody relaxed. I tossed up whether I should go back because I was starting to feel pretty exhausted, and I still couldn't see the top of the hill. Ego kept nudging. *Manly's at sea level, you know*, he was saying. *The further uphill you go now, the bigger the hill you have to face coming up from the beach on the home journey.*

But I kept going. I had to. I'd phoned Laurie to tell him I was going to Manly, so there was no way I could back out of finishing it.

By the time I reached Manly I was leg-sore and weary all over. Now I knew exactly how tough things must be for Diggers on the Kokoda Trail. They had jungle and century temperatures, humidity, sweat, and disease to cope with as well, but I knew they could never be as exhausted as I felt. I was even too tired to go into the surf. The clouds had come over anyway, and rain was threatening.

You should be starting for home, Ego kept urging.

Oh how I wished I could fall into a sleep and wake up already home and in my bed. And ploughing up the hill to reach the crest, my legs just felt they'd never get through the next revolution of the sprocket wheel, let alone the thirteen miles home. Even after getting to the crest of this hill, I still had that long, curving hill the other side of the bridge to face.

Would they let me take my bike on a tram, even if I had to pay double?

Ego was doubtful. *But you could stop a tram and ask*, he said. But then when I thought of the grins and giggles on the faces of the tram passengers as I hauled my bike aboard, that put paid to that bright idea.

And if there should be any boy from school on the tram, Ego, it would make it doubly insufferable. I'd have to change schools.

And will I ever remember that dreadful haul up the other side from the Spit Bridge—absolute agony for every muscle in my legs and back! And mind, what made it worse was that I simply couldn't get out of my head the memory of how great it was on the out journey to be able to freewheel all the way down.

But I made it. I knew my body had never been more stressed. And the hardest part was trying not to let anybody see how much pain I was in. I breathed in pretty hard when I saw Mum was home before me.

"Hello, darling," she said. "I was thinking of you on your long ride. How did it go?"

"Oh, pretty good. I had a good day. And the surf was fine."

But as I crawled into bed straight after dinner I swore I would never do something like that again.

Like General MacArthur, I told Ego, *I'll get maps and plot my next campaign more carefully.*

~ * ~

In the greatest battle the Middle East had ever witnessed, Aussie's Rats of Tobruk, as they were dubbed, finally kicked the Germans out of El Alamein and started them on their retreat back to Algiers.

Aussies fighting on the Kokoda Trail on Papua's north coast were trying to drive the Japs off the beach but weren't having as much success as their brothers in Africa.

"Many Aussies killed or wounded in fierce jungle fighting," we were told.

"Bloody hell," I said to Laurie. Bloody Papua New Guinea was our nearest island—only a strait between them and us, no wider than the English Channel!

Things were really looking grim.

If they can get airports in Papua, they'll soon be bombing us.

I wrote to General MacArthur, addressing it c/o Australian Army Headquarters, asking why don't we simply drop swarms of funnel-web spiders or even better, taipans, deadliest snake in the world of which Australia had plenty, into Jap camps. Far less costly, I told him, than risking Aussie lives in combat. He never replied, so I was left with the perpetual wonder of whether or not he'd received it.

But there was also, now, another urgent problem.

My air raid shelter was collapsing. I hadn't allowed for rain seeping into it, and during the winter some three or four feet of water had built up. Even the steps down to it were by now nowt but a slithery mudslide. Mrs. Rowling downstairs thought it funny, but I couldn't see the joke. There was no seat any more; that entire earth shelf had slithered away. I couldn't see how badly, because it was all under water.

Where would we find safety now if the air raid sirens began to wail? The worst part of it was that to start again, build another one, the same thing would happen. I couldn't work out why mine failed and Uncle Eric's was still fine. I was just so pleased I'd never told him I was building one; otherwise he'd have asked me, in turn, how mine was going.

Scouts were co-opted to help with coast-watching. Those of us with bicycles were stationed along the foreshores of Sydney Harbour from sundown until 9 p.m., when we were relieved by seniors so we could go home to sleep before school come morning.

So I had real pressures on my time now.

Wednesday afternoon I went straight from school to Gran's to do her shopping. She would have me write out what she wanted because I had trouble reading her 'squiggly' writing as I called it. And she was pretty fussy in the way she wanted her vegetables. She didn't want potatoes with lots of nobbles on them. And if the pumpkin weren't a nice bright orange in colour then I was to buy parsnips instead. And I was to be sure to tell the butcher that what I was buying was for Mrs. Mitchell because he knew exactly how thick she liked her lamb loin-chops—and how much fat she was prepared to accept on them. "Too fatty, my boy," she would tell me, "you'll have to take them back and get cutlets instead." But the groceries were easier. There was no mucking about with packaged things. And I had my experience of serving in Reecy's shop to know something of how different products were sold.

And if butter were on the list, it being, like cheese, a product delivered from the wholesalers in bulk to be weighed out like sugar and meat, I had to be sure of doing the meat and green-grocery shopping first, else the butter, the amount you wanted wrapped in greaseproof paper, would melt before I could get it home. But I knew about all that. I'd learned it when doing Aunt Grace's shopping at Northbridge.

At Northbridge, however, the way home with all the shopping was down a steep hill. At Naremburn, it was Gran who lived atop a steep hill and the shops by the tram-stop at the bottom. So it was an uphill climb with a laden bike, reminiscent of the bloody hills on the road to Manly—but only a tiny fraction of the distance.

Gran's house was old and little—old enough that electricity stopped at one power point per room. The bath heater was wood-chip, like the laundry copper, although the bathroom at least had a board floor. All the lighting in the house, ceiling lamps and wall sconces, were fuelled by piped gas, so my last job every Wednesday was to climb up on her dining room table to light the lamp. She was able to turn it off by reaching up with her walking stick to hook the handle into the on-off ring-pull—a sort of rocker switch.

"What do you do when I'm not here to turn it on, Gran? Sit in the dark and just listen to the wireless?"

"Yes, lad," she had replied, "quite often."

~ * ~

Mum arrived home one evening to report that Mr. Gould's shop was closed up and had a sign on the shutter saying the business had closed. He'd said nothing to me last Saturday.

"What else did the sign say?"

"Nothing else."

I wasn't satisfied with such a bland answer. I'd still been giving Mum two-and-six out of my four bob, leaving me with one-and-six "to indulge your desires on" as Mum always joked, but now I'd have nowt. I got on my bike and went around to the shop. It looked so forlorn. I was so used to mounds of greens and wallowing in the smells of cantaloupe that ever abounded—my most favourite smell ever. But sure enough, that's all the sign said. The business had closed. I went next door to the deli and asked what they knew about it.

"This morning, two military policemen came. We heard loud voices, then they pulled down the shutters. They watched while he put the padlocks on, then took him away in an army van."

Well! What was I to make of that?

"Could he have been a spy for the Germans or Japs?" I asked.

The lady laughed. "He couldn't even add up his takings without a slide-rule," she said. "I can't see him being clever enough to be a spy."

I had never thought anyone had to be clever to be a spy—just careful about keeping secrets seemed a reasonable qualification. But he'd gone, and time was to prove we'd never see or hear of him again. Roy thought he might have been a 'draft-dodger' and was now being sent off to the war.

And there was another problem: Roy moved out.

Mum's younger sister Elsie was also a widow, living only a street away with her young daughter. Mum made the mistake, as it turned out, of introducing her to Roy, and now he'd changed his lodgings to Aunt Elsie's flat.

"They're getting married," said Mum.

Then she dropped the real clanger: "And so am I. I've promised to marry Lou Somers."

Well, as if the Mr. Gould thing hadn't been surprise enough, without all this.

"Will we live in the house on Sirius Cove?"

My mind flew to that night with the torpedoes exploding, sirens blaring and searchlights blinding us. But where would I keep my bike? I couldn't get it up and down all those steps...

"No, he'll come and live here."

Mum, Val, and I then sat and talked a long time,

Mum said she'd been very lonely, also that Lou, quite some years older than she, we reckoned, was also lonely and that both would be happier if having each other. And neither he nor Mum wanted the problem of all those steps as they got older. He would sell his house, give some of the money to his married daughters, but would keep enough that our new family could live comfortably enough that Mum wouldn't have to work.

"So Val gets her room back, and for you, Kev, Lou is going to build-in the veranda with proper windows to make it a better room for you."

Well, that would be good. During winters, the blinds let in cold draughts.

"What will we call him?"

I wasn't keen on the idea of calling him 'Dad.'

"We talked about that," Mum said. "He wants to be Pop Somers to you kids, so you can call him Pop. He says he's looking forward to having a boy around for the first time in his life. And he'll surely be a good man to have around when you start Architectural School. He was a master building contractor by trade, you know, same as Uncle Eric. And he has a car."

All in all, Ego whispered, *this adds up to being a pretty good thing all round.*

Except, answered I, *that this is the end of getting meat for dinner on Fridays, and I hate fish!*

I liked the guy otherwise, though. He was a quieter bloke than Dad, sort of not as outgoing. But I reckoned we should get along all right.

Just to show Mum how good we felt about it, Val and I pooled pocket money enough to buy her a Vera Lynn record so she could sing along with her whenever she wanted. We didn't have the big gramophone—Mum had sold that to Reecy before leaving Brisbane. But we had a portable.

Nine

Things were really happening in Africa. The Aussies had the Germans on the run, driving them west from Egypt; in the far northwest, Algerian and Moroccan forces rose against the Vichy French government to support the Allies. Hitler appointed Rommel, his best man, to regain lost ground.

"But Monty's got his measure, Pop," I told Lou Somers.

"General Montgomery to you, boy. But yes, he seems to be doing well there. I heard yesterday that the Americans have landed marines in North Africa, so that can only help.

"'Jerry is finding his African foothold slippery,' is what the wireless said this morning."

Pop kept well up with things in the war. He was proving a good ally. He would even make notes to tell me about things he'd heard during the day. So that was pretty good.

In Papua-New Guinea, the Americans were supplying our men with equipment. We didn't have much of our own. The Aussie Air Force was given Kittyhawks and trained by US pilots, and they were proving mighty helpful in holding back the Japs. Biggest problem was that Japan seemed to have countless millions of troops. Aussie forces were small by comparison, despite the government was calling up older men. But we had the advantage in the jungles.

"Japs aren't used to hot weather and jungle conditions," we were told. "So given the right equipment, we are making a better fist of holding back their advance."

Holding back their advance? Holding back their bloody advance…?

"What bloody balderdash these news reporters talk! Holding back their advance only means they're still making ground and we're still retreating! Why can't they say what they mean?"

"They're trying to keep up our morale," Pop said. "They have to read what's given to them to read—that's their job. If they kept telling us 'We're still retreating,' there would be panic. All we can do is do our best."

But I could see he was really worried. When studying my map wondering what could possibly stop them landing in Oz, New Guinea looked so close that I could almost hear their guns blazing. With the Philippines in their path, that had offered some visible sign of a barrier, but when it became only the East Indies, the barrier wasn't even significant. And now, with both those lands in Japanese hands, on paper they were now ready to pounce on us. It now seemed right down to hand-to-hand fighting, and here we were outnumbered a thousand to one.

My heart went out to the bravery our boys were showing, and the more I thought about it the more I could see how wrong it would be for the government to be telling these boys' mothers that their sons were not doing the job so essential in saving us all.

~ * ~

We had chook for Christmas. We never saw chicken these days, but Mum was able to get an old-mother-hen as she called it from neighbours who had been told both their sons had been killed in action "somewhere to the north;" they were quitting their house to go live with one of their now widowed daughters-in-law and her children. They were selling off the fowls that had been supplying eggs to others in our street, and Mum ended up with this old 'boiler.'

"Had to boil it for hours before I could bake it," she told us, "just to get it tender enough to eat."

But it tasted great to me. I couldn't remember ever having eaten chicken.

"It would have been when we lived in Brisbane," Mum said.

So it was quite a treat.

My old scooter, stowed under the stairs since getting my pushbike, I gave to young John Rowling downstairs for Christmas.

"It's simply going to waste under those stairs," Mum had said. "When Millie Rowling's having trouble scraping up enough coin to feed the two of them, she cannot buy him a Christmas present."

So I told young John that I heard his mother had sold some jewellery so she could buy the scooter, and that seemed to make him happy.

There was the best of news ever, though, early in the New Year. The Allies had at last broken the German code for U-boats in the Atlantic. Whilst this was never reported in case it got back to the Germans, who would then have introduced a new code, Pop Somers reckoned that that is what must have happened.

"It's pretty obvious how all of a sudden, after a year or more of hearing of all the losses of cargo ships crossing the Atlantic, we are now getting reports of how many U-boats are being sunk. And I would guess that every day we are getting aeroplanes with longer range, so that the Atlantic Black Hole is shrinking."

When I sat over my maps I could see what he meant. With my now tech-drawing lessons coupled with trigonometry, I could graph out how quickly the hole would shrink for every extra mile our air surveillance could cover. So it was now U-boats that were having a hard time of it rather than vital supply ships for Britain.

But I still scratched my head over Iceland. Why Hitler was even interested in taking the war to Africa, other than to take the Suez Canal, I couldn't fathom. Why didn't he instead, concentrate on taking Iceland?

Val was in her last year of high school—it was only four years for girls while five for boys—and she was chuffed when made a prefect.

Now it had been clear to me that school prefects were nowt but spies appointed by schools to spy on kids not doing the right things. I reckoned it was the same thing our history master had said about Germany's *Gestapo*. It was simply restricting our freedom. If we were planning some escapade, such as giving Old Crusty a drenching, it always had to be a case of keeping it secret from prefects—which all added up to them being sneaky people. So why should my sister be so proud of becoming one?

And that thought led to another. *Next*, I said to Ego, *our government will likely introduce tough-armed men like Hitler's Black Shirts, who were pretty mean characters. They proved that the way they took to Germany's Jews.*

But the family talk over dinner was all now on what sort of job Val might get after school. I couldn't see the sense of why we should worry about it now when it was only March. There were still eight months before exam time.

Rationing kept getting worse. Instead of putting prices up, they just kept increasing the number of coupons needed, so you could buy less—a sneaky way of making it harder to eat well. Bread wasn't rationed, which was one good thing—Australia having more wheat than any other country in the world, we learned at school—so we still ate well at breakfast. That was, of course, if you didn't like butter. There was always Vegemite, however, and the government knew there'd be riots if they tried rationing that. But why we had to have coupons for butter I had no idea. It wasn't as if it could be sent to England, despite they told us that's what they were doing. Surely it would be rotten before it ever got there. I was ever getting into trouble just leaving butter out of our fridge for even a minute.

But we were luckier than most. Mum swapped our sugar coupons for Aunt Ida's butter coupons. We didn't eat much sugar in our house, and Aunt Ida's sister had a farm and made her own butter, so sent her coupons to Ida.

It was eggs we missed most.

"It's because we ate that hen for Christmas," Mum joked. And Pop would laugh at that. There were so many little ways that Val and I could tell how much happier Mum was since marrying Pop. And he seemed satisfied enough with his new family—except when it came down to petrol coupons. He'd got rid of the big gas-bag from on top of his old Dodge because with it the car couldn't get into the garage, and he'd found a garage to rent behind the house opposite. If you didn't keep cars in a garage these days, things would get stolen off it—tyres or windscreen wipers that, like spare parts for my bike, didn't get made any more. And petrol would get syphoned out of the tank by robbers, because petrol was so severely rationed.

The car was an old Dodge tourer with lift-out windows that leaked in really heavy rain—and they'd get stolen, too, from cars left unguarded at night. Older than me, the car was. "But we've got to take care of it because cars are something else you can't buy new any more."

Pop mixed his petrol with what he called Power-Kero, a special sort of kerosene he could get without coupons that if mixed with petrol in the right proportions gave the engine enough power without blowing too much smoke out the exhaust—except when going up-hill, we found. So sometimes he would take a different route, albeit longer, rather than risk getting caught for mixing this concoction. Why, I didn't know, and when I asked why it should be illegal, he just told me that should be left as his secret.

"Just don't tell anyone else I do it, eh?"

So I knew it was either illegal or dangerous or something. So I kept his secret, even from friends like Laurie and Alan.

Alan was another friend I had to keep secrets about.

His Mum was yet another old friend of Mum's. I always reckoned my mum had more friends than anyone else. It had ever amazed me. Most people collected a few during their lives, but Mum had them on strings, it seemed. She and Pop were taking off for the Easter break for a holiday in Katoomba, up in the mountains west of Sydney. They'd been there for their honeymoon, and I got the feeling they felt a bit like Val and Nelson Eddy about the place—romantic stuff and all that.

"Val can go stay with Sue down at Balmoral. How would you like to go stay with Alan up at Hornsby?"

Ah, I thought, *why can't I go stay with Laurie?* But I'd wait and see why she'd picked on Alan. I realised, of course, that this would have already been arranged so it didn't really matter whether it was Alan I wanted to stay with or not. But I couldn't say so without starting an argument.

"Mrs. Browne is always asking me to come stay some time," I tossed by way of a subtle hint. But again Mum had a "kill that" answer on the tip of her tongue.

"Because Alan's ma rang me and asked if you could stay over Easter. She likes you too, you know. And this was so timely, Pop and me were already thinking of going to Katoomba."

Gees, a kid can never bloody win. They've always got things organised to suit themselves.

"Who's 'they'?" Val asked when I posed this to her.

"Parents. Parents in general." I could see she realised I was in a pique.

"Well, consider yourself lucky they think of us. Some parents would just go off and leave us fend for ourselves."

I could have made a quip but knew it was useless. There was nowt I could do about it but say 'Yes.'

It was too far to ride my bike to Alan's, even further than Manly! I went by train. Hornsby was the far north of Sydney's suburbs, where the mountains started—the range that made the road so difficult between Sydney and Newcastle. From Hornsby station I had to take a bus, and even at that, there was a fair walk to the house along a bush track. The Addams had a car that even Mrs. Addams drove. I didn't know any other woman who could drive. The house was so isolated that she even had to take Alan and Cilla to school every day—and pick them up.

"She takes it in turn with Mrs. Brixton, who also has kids," Alan had told me.

All the way I wondered what I was heading for. Alan was all right. He was a year older than me, and a Scout, so we had that in common. And his parents were all right in their way. His mum was as organised a lady as mine; that's why Alan and I got on together, we reckoned—

we understood each other's difficulties. His dad was a bank manager at Hornsby who would drive the car in with the family each morning so Mrs. Addams could then drop the kids at school, do her shopping, then take the car home. They did this day-about with their only neighbours, the Brixtons. Mr. Brixton was an architect. I had seen their house, and it was pretty neat—lots of glass, and it had a flat roof. It was perched right on the edge of a mountain, with great bush views. He was now something to do with the war so was away somewhere.

As the journey progressed, I became more satisfied. *If I'm not enjoying it*, I told myself, *I can make an excuse and come home. I have my key.* I'd learned, by now, to always look for the good side of things when in a shitty mood. There usually was a good side to things if one looked hard enough. Or so Ego kept telling me.

And Cilla? Alan's sister? Same age as me, with lots of freckles. I didn't like freckled girls—didn't like girls much at all, in fact. Dreary, they were. Boys were better mates, freckled or not.

Their house was nice, big, and bang in the middle of bush where there were thousands of kookaburras. Drive you mad, they did, with their noise. Yet a nice noise.

Maybe if we get into the bush a bit, I thought, *things will be okay.* I liked bushwalking.

~ * ~

Mrs. Addams made a fuss of me.

"Oh," she said, "I was so happy for your ma when she married her Lou. I know she was lonely..."

Yes, I thought, lonely—and finding it tough to get by. I just had that feeling that Mum must have married just to get out of that bind. Why else would she choose someone so unlike Dad? If she had to choose at all, that is.

"...Life is not easy these days, Kev..."

I hated being called Kev. I was Ric by now to most people I knew, except family. Family seemed to insist on Kev. But then, Ego kept prompting that Mrs. Addams was sort of family.

"...A woman alone in time of war has nowhere to turn with all the new troubles we get confronted with."

But Mum had never been alone. She had Val and me. But I had to hear this out. She wanted to say these things, so I let her ramble on. But when she obviously felt she'd said all the dutiful things, she told me I was welcome and that I should look forward to having a happy Easter.

"Alan has things planned, I know. He and his friends have a bush-house in the scrub. They keep it secret so even I don't know exactly where it is. And I know he wants you to see it."

They too lived on the side of a hill with great bush views. In the valley below was a little river, Alan had told me—wasn't even a track down to there, let alone a road. My mind shrugged. Maybe things would work out.

Alan was up the back of the property feeding the fowls—they had something like a thousand. It was Alan's job every day to feed them. That's how his mum had me captive when I arrived.

I wanted to know how interested Alan was in the war and if his parents were keen on listening to the news. But that hope was to turn out for the worst. They didn't listen to war news at all.

"We like to think that here in the bush is not part of the rat-race out there. Our bush environment is sacred, not part of the crazy world. Mr. Addams gets his fill of that at work, but we try not to let its problems invade our home..."

I smiled inside. It was likely, I reckoned, that if the Japs did invade, they'd never even find this house.

"...When it comes to the war we can change nothing, so why bother about it?" Mrs Addams continued. "If we need to start taking precautionary actions, Mr. Addams will be told at work. Meanwhile we just carry on enjoying what we have."

Well! Had anyone ever heard such unpatriotic words? I was horrified.

When Alan and I went to bed that night, he sleeping on the floor of his room so I could have the bed, we talked about the war. I could quickly tell how little of it he knew.

I was aghast! What sort of Easter was I going to spend? The bloody Japs could be settling on our north coast and I wouldn't even know!

Alan and I talked on and on about did I like girls and that sort of rubbish while all the important things in life were cast off like blowflies at a barbie. They always kept coming back of course. It seemed that no matter how hard I tried to make my point clear on things, Alan seemed to parry every one. I'd never realised how two people could have such opposite views on something so important.

It must have made me happy to drift off into sleep that night.

Ten

After breakfast Alan and Cilla did what appeared daily chores in the almost self-sufficient little farm the family had within fences—fences high enough only to keep marauding little creatures from eating the vegetables. And they had the biggest aviary I'd ever seen, filled with a veritable rainbow of bright finches in all sorts of sizes. And two large Alsatians that fortunately seemed to like me.

"They like all our friends," Cilla told me. "They can sense if someone is our friend. If not, then they're on guard. That's why Mum and Dad don't worry about us taking to the bush alone. They know, somehow, that if we're in trouble, Tiffy the bitch will stay with us while Taffy races home for help."

We were all quickly at ease. Even Alan's and Cilla's freckles weren't worrying me. Their entire complexion, I hadn't realised before, had more than a hint of ginger.

"C'mon over to the Brixtons' house. We'll see if they've got anything planned," said Alan.

There was no made road for cars into the houses, only wheel-tracks through hand-hewn bush. "Our 'homemade' road," Mr. Addams had described it over dinner when discussing their isolation. It was even some two or three hundred yards to their only neighbour. Each had its car-track twisting around trees until it reached the bitumen road where the bus ran. A proper 'street' was in the town plan, but building it was 'on the shelf' until after the war. Town water was connected, and temporary telephone and electric wiring was strung between trees.

"After the war," Mr Addams added, "when the street is built, all those services will be underground."

And the Brixton kids seemed okay. Twins Roger and Amanda were Alan's age, and Paul the same as Cilla and me—so only a year separated all six.

"We're thinking of going to the humpy," Cilla told them. You want to come?"

They looked at each other for a second before sizing me up. Then all smiled. "Yeah, we'll come. Give us thirty minutes, and we'll meet you at the track."

"We've built a humpy between us down the track a-way," said Alan as we walked back home. "We'll grab some bubbly to drink, make some sandwiches, then take you to see it. It's where we kids go to have fun."

"Good. I'll be in that."

We collected two bottles of homemade ginger beer and made sandwiches.

"Mugs and plates are already there. We don't need anything else."

"Will I need a hat?"

"Nah. It's in thick bush everywhere."

"Far?"

"Enough."

We waited for the Brixton kids where a little-worn track branched off. They had brought drinks and fruit. Tiffy and Taffy were one minute running ahead and the next running behind, checking out every tree, shrub, and insect. But they kept us in their sights.

It was a good thirty minutes, I reckon, certainly well off any other track.

"We like things private," they said, laughing.

"You like games?" Amanda asked.

"I'm easy about most things. What sort of games?"

"Cops and Robbers, Cowboys and Indians, Goodies and Baddies," said Roger.

Alan laughed. "We make games up on the spur of the minute. Things we can play with even or odd numbers. Doesn't matter, really."

"We don't even have rules," said Cilla.

They all seemed easygoing about everything.

And the humpy was well named. It was little more than twigs with some canvas over the top to keep rain out. The ground around it was well-trodden earth, and the bush around it privately thick.

"The dogs ensure our safety. They give plenty of warning of anyone coming."

No one else would ever find the way, I heard Ego muttering.

Roger brought a tin from the humpy, filled with oddments of twigs by the look of it. He counted out six, four long and two short. He put these into the tin and tapped the straw heads into his palm so all looked, from what we could see, the same length. He held it towards me...

"Want to draw a straw?"

I looked at Alan...

"Yeah, just pick one," he said with an offhand grin.

I drew a long one.

So did Cilla.

Paul drew a short one.

Alan a long one

All but Roger laughed, then. "Ah, I get the other short one. Looks like you and me are the Baddies, Paul."

Nobody seemed disappointed, however. They'd obviously played the game many times, for none had questions. There were many in my mind of course, but I wouldn't ask. I didn't want to be seen as a scaredy-cat.

Paul went into the humpy and brought out two coils of thin rope.

Alan put his hands on his hips and stared me straight in the eyes.

"I've put my reputation on the line here," he said. "I told them you'd be in anything no matter how quirky."

"Quirky?" I couldn't help but ask this question.

"Yeah. A game you've not played before. Cilla and me talked about it, and we reckon you are right for it."

I looked at Cilla, and she nodded. I had to trust them.

"You can play on my side, she said. "That means Alan and Amanda are partners."

"Four Goodies and two Baddies?"

"Yes. We Goodies play in pairs."

It didn't make sense. Roger had complained about his short straw making him a Baddie.

But you're committed now, whatever happens, whispered Ego.

"Come in the humpy, Ric."

I followed Cilla inside, mind whirling with so many unanswered questions. The humpy walls were anything but private, simply haphazard twigs and dried leaves that left holes everywhere. From inside you could see out and from outside you could, to a certain extent, see in.

The dogs were already asleep by the entrance.

"Take your shoes off, Ric. And your shirt."

And she started taking her own things off...

Oh, oh... A tingle ran through me. But I wasn't going to back out. Boys at school talked about games that called for boys and girls with clothes off. And every kid had seemed happy about what happened. I'd simply thought it a game that I'd probably never experience. But Goodies and Baddies? And four boys and two girls? And only walls people could see through?

I took my shoes off, and shirt. So did Cilla, to come straight to me to rub her little but budding breasts against me.

Ahhh! I really tingled now.

But she backed straight off again and pointed through the wall. Roger and Paul were as naked as the day they were born!

Amanda and Alan were not only stripped as far as Cilla and me, but Alan was now taking his shorts off.

Oh dear God! My mouth gaped.

Cilla was watching me, I was conscious, to see what I would do. So I took a deep, deep breath, then took my shorts off. Cilla was in only her nickers and starting to pull them down even as I watched.

"All the way," she said.

Ahhhhh! I knew I was getting hard. One side of Ego's mouth seemed to be telling me to back down, but the other was saying, *Be in it, Ric. Look through the wall there—all three boys are now naked and all have erections. You can't back out now. Just keep your cool and let them lead you.*

It's all right for you, I told it. *It's not your cock sticking out.*

I just felt so embarrassed. Yet the other side of my mind flew to the pangs of envy when at school, listening to those guys talking about their 'initiations.' *And learning about girls has got to start some time! And I've three other guys here giving moral support. It's not as if I'm alone with a girl. And at least I know the girl, and she knows what I'm going through.*

I had never seen a girl naked. I knew what to expect but to suddenly be confronted with it was frightening, I discovered. I knew she knew I was staring at her, yet she just stood there, smiling and eyeing me up and down.

Oh, there is just so much I don't know of the world—I've seen boys naked but only when changing in the gym or in the sheds at the pool; but that's when it's all only boys. And all boys know the worst thing that could happen is to have an erection when it's only boys about.

But here?

"Come on, let's join the others. You've got to help tie up the Baddies."

My erection grew full on, and my heart nearly slumped as she grabbed my hand and pulled me outside.

"These are our whipping trees," said Alan, pointing at two particular trees. Then he put me right on the spot by pointing out my erection to all the others.

I nearly died—but tried to compose myself...

"Wh—whipping trees?"

Amanda Brixton didn't even blush as she sidled over with mock humility and clasped my swollen privates. I nearly peaked on the spot.

"You really are cute," she said, leaning up to kiss me, taking one of my hands and planting it on her little breast.

"Feel my heart."

She held my hand there for what seemed an eternity of desperately trying self-control. I nearly died with embarrassment.

Or is it ecstasy? asked Ego.

We all were stark naked, and I helped rope Roger and Paul to their respective trees, not tightly, legs and torsos securely fastened but arms left swinging free.

"We sometimes whip with some of this rope," Alan tossed off as if talking about the weather, "but never hard. Last thing we want is any of us going home with red welts."

"Don't either of your parents have any idea?"

All shook their heads.

"Do you think my mother would let us out of her sight ever again if they did?" Amanda pulled a shocked face as she said it, and her brothers giggled.

"And ours," added Cilla.

"And the dogs tell no tales," said Alan.

"So what happens now?"

All looked at me, obviously happy that I was at least, for the time being, being swept along without fighting back.

Alan answered. "Have you ever done anything like this before?"

"Never in all my born days! I've never, until now, seen a girl naked."

"You like what you see?" Cilla laughed—as did all the others at her quip.

"Yes, but I can't help feeling embarrassed."

"We'll fix that. Just bear with us," Alan answered.

I was finding it hard to 'just bear' with them. I was terrified I would disgrace myself.

He went to the humpy to bring a large blanket—the blanket I'd used to lay my clothes on. He shook dried leaves and things from it and spread it on the ground in front of Roger and Paul, who still had erections. Alan, I noticed, had begun to lose his...

Could this mean I shouldn't be harbouring so much fear?

Yet I knew the respite couldn't last. It would depend on what would happen, of course—although I was beginning to get the idea.

Alan then handed me one of two condoms he'd had hidden in a hand.

"Try this for size. Cilla will help you."

Ahhhh again. I pleaded with Ego to help me.

Everybody else was laughing.

Cilla helped me. I prayed to every God of every religion I could think of that I could control myself. My fingers were fumbling while hers seemed practised.

Amanda was lying herself down on the blanket. Cilla then flopped beside her. Alan knelt down over Amanda...

...Cilla beckoned me to do the same...

Right beside each other? And in full view of Roger and Paul? Oh, dear God!

I prayed to Ego again, and I was vaguely conscious of one of the dogs yawning.

All the rest happened so quickly—every emotion was an awakening, an introduction to an entire new world. I remembered later wondering what on earth would have happened if the short straws had fallen differently. Surely those brothers and sister wouldn't... I did indeed find out later, on asking. No, they never did.

And on the walk home I asked why Roger and Paul had been called the Baddies. "Because they were the two with bad luck," I was told.

But oh—what an adventure had that day brought!

Never again could 'young Ric' claim innocence.

Was this, then, the start of me becoming a man?

I somehow felt grateful to all of them, especially Cilla. Oh what a hurdle in life I had finally cleared!

~ * ~

After it I began wondering, naturally enough, what Val and Sue might be doing on their weekend tryst at Balmoral.

Surely my sister wouldn't…

No. Every time I wondered on it I could only feel confident that my dear Valerie satisfied herself with sighing over Nelson Eddy on the screen. Somehow when it came to imagining Val doing something like this it seemed dirty—tarnished in a sort of way. I hadn't felt it that way, yet how would Val have seen it?

I couldn't help but feel it was all part of discovering about life, and how lucky was I that it was Cilla rather than someone to make me feel bad.

But put it aside, Ric, I told myself with a mental slap on the wrist. *There's life to be lived.*

"Didn't you hear what I said?"

My presence clicked back in. Val and I were washing dishes. Mum and Pop had settled in the living room in front of the fire, listening to Dad and Dave.

I hated drying. It was so utterly boring. Washing, except on Sundays when dinner was roast something with greasy baking dishes and gravy spills on everything else, was easy provided you whisked up enough suds with the soap-saver. So in a way, I envied people in England who were next to starving. They at least would have easier wash-ups.

I had a new job. Mum and Pop were agreed that until September when I'd have to knuckle down in earnest swatting for late November exams, I should keep doing Gran's shopping on Wednesdays but do deliveries the other four days. Mr. Frazer had the chemist shop at Crows Nest junction—right opposite the enlistment office that every week, it seemed, had older and older men waiting to be sent to some glorious death.

In the block of flats next door, Mr. and Mrs. Gordon went every winter Saturday to the Rugby League matches. North Sydney, our local team, never in my time won the Sydney competition but was always in with a hopeful chance. The biggest lesson I learned from this period of my life was that it was always possible to believe that Next Year things must be better. We relived that hope every year—without fail. Mr. Gordon was in the Air Force, although I think he never got near an aeroplane and remained careful to somehow engineer that he had every Saturday free for footy. And he seemed never concerned that he might be sent away. My mum used to say he was a better organiser, by far, than she ever had been.

So while Val was re-arranging Nelson Eddy pin-ups on the laundry walls because Mum wouldn't have them 'cluttering up' the house, I'd go to the footy with the Gordons. Mick was allowed to have his wife in the jeep, but not other civilians, so every week I travelled to and fro on the floor in back under a rug. Many times I was conscious, trapped down there and unable to see out, of my tummy feeling much as it did in the back of motor cars on windy roads. Mick Gordon always wore his uniform so never had to pay bridge toll, and he was often given a discount on entering the home ground, depending whether or not a mate was on the turnstile that day.

Often, of course, we never knew who would be playing in our team. Pretty well all the team were servicemen without cushy jobs like Mick's. Sometimes they disappeared and it was a year or more before we saw them run on to the field again. They'd always get a great cheer from those watching on those occasions.

When my old school-case collapsed, Pop made me a new one. You couldn't buy them any more. What he made was the most sophisticated of all in school. It was a Christmas present. With all the homework I was beginning to get I sometimes had hefty loads, so the case had to be strong. I'd always wished NSW schools had the sensible back-strap ports that Queensland kids used, but NSW would never admit that Queensland could teach the older state anything. Pop found some plywood from somewhere and fitted up a wooden case with proper metal corners and proper clip closers. And it was all glossy with lacquer. I didn't take the bike to school any more because I had too many books every day. I would meet up with lots of mates at the tram-stop and, for a long time after getting my new case, got ragged by all and sundry because I had, without doubt, the best sparkling case of any kid.

"It's the best in all North Tech," I told Pop.

~ * ~

In Africa, in May, Tunisia fell to the Allies. On the Russian front, the Krauts were on the run. They finally gave up trying to take Leningrad and Stalingrad, both of which, by now, were nowt but piles of rubble.

In July the HMAS *Hobart*, same as had been bombed by the United States in the Coral Sea last year, was torpedoed by a Japanese submarine. Many lives were lost, including our neighbour, Mr. Rowling. My mum spent not just hours but many days trying to pacify Millie Rowling after the dreaded telegram arrived. The *Hobart* had limped home to Sydney's Cockatoo Island dockyards for repairs minus several score seamen and officers.

In the Mediterranean Sea the Allies invaded Italy. They landed in Sicily, and the Italians, despite it was their own country, again showed their lack of mettle when it came to fighting. The big island fell quickly, and it wasn't long before a landing was made on the mainland at Salerno near Naples—or Napoli as the Ities call it. Italy was almost on the brink of a civil war. It seemed there were as many believed that the Allies would win the war as those who still sided with Germany.

"The Italians continue advancing backwards," insisted the wags. So the Germans took a hand. They flooded troops that had fled Russia into Italy. But no sooner had they begun moving south did Italy renounce its alliance with Germany. It changed sides, formerly declaring war on Germany.

Wait on... I rushed for Pop's encyclopaedias—he had a whole set of them, and in them a kid could find everything he needed to know.

I had in mind that I'd read somewhere how Italy did that same thing during the First World War. When they saw that Germany was losing, they changed sides. Cute, I thought. Cute? Dare I even think it? It was 'cute' that Amanda Brixton called me when I was naked.

Ahhhh—those memories! But I could never tell a soul—except Laurie. We were best mates and told each other everything. Oh! He was just so envious!

And yes, the Ities had done it then, too—just needed to be on the winning side.

But it wasn't clever thinking. Despite they captured Hitler's friend Mussolini and threw him into prison, the country had suddenly become full of Germans who were against the change, of course. Those who had been friends yesterday were suddenly enemies.

Oh! How fickle is war, I concluded. Here was every village in Italy at war with neighbours, all at once. The Ities were not very bright, I began to realise.

So it was now not the weak Italians our forces had to contend with in Italy; it was the strong Germans. The Italians said they would help us fight, but I reckon they were told to quietly go and harass the Germans on their own and leave the serious stuff to Aussies and Americans.

~ * ~

Football season seemed always the busiest.

I played rugger in the North Shore Scouts Competition on most Sundays—mornings as a rule, except for the first Sunday every month. That's when every Scout had to attend mock battlefields for first aid classes.

'Practising for War' we called it. Every first Sunday, every Sydney suburban park was strewn with prostrate 'bodies' while housewives, mothers, Scouts, and Girl-Guides made free with their arms, legs, heads, and every part of a body that could get injured—every part but one, we kids used to snigger behind shielding palms. Kids as young as three and four were taught by older ones how to roll bandages. This was great training for Scouts going for their Ambulance badges, of course. The organisation was immense. Whoever was the person organising it all had my total admiration. I only hoped they had a say in how the war was being run.

But all in all, it pointed to the fact that we would be reasonably well organised when the bombers did come over.

Eleven

I began new adventures. I had always had a yen for outdoor living, ever since childhood in Queensland, where Dad would take me to the mudflats at Sandgate to catch crabs. And I'm not talking about small crabs but 'bloody big ones.' That's what Dad called them.

And so easy to catch.

We'd lie on the end of a wharf with fish-bait tied to a length of line—even string—and wait until we could tell we had a Queensland muddy grasping at the bait. The idea was to gently raise the line until the crab, still nibbling happily away, broke the surface. Then we'd slide a long-handled net under it. A few quick twists of the wrist soon had the muddy entangled enough to land him. Getting him into our sack, of course, was a painfully learnt skill, but Dad had obviously passed the test. We would come home with a big haul.

Only way to cook such big crabs, when so many, was to have outdoors a four-gallon can of water bubbling over a strong fire. Dad would poke out an eye of each crab with the garden fork, which penetrated their brain to have them quickly dead, to then chuck them into boiling water. Wow! I've loved crabmeat ever since. And barbies.

Scout Camps, for me, proved a delight, but they were held so seldom.

At school, however, I discovered a whole new love of camping. And surfing.

Music Master Neville Meal, who was quickly nick-named Old Mealy despite he was the only young teacher in school, only about twenty or something when all others were old codgers, had the head's okay to every other weekend take a half dozen or so boys camping. Why he wasn't away in the war I never asked, because if he had not been still at school, I'd never have discovered this side benefit to life.

The big NSW National Park south of Sydney could be reached by electric train. It took several days to walk through it north-south or east-west, and we did both on different occasions. Selected kids would, with our gear, meet at North Sydney Station, directly opposite the school, on the Friday evening. I would arrange for another friend on these occasion, maybe once every two months or so as my turn came around, to sub for me delivering Mr. Frazer's prescriptions.

Nev Meal's camping trips beat Scout camps hands down because there was no need for the hundred percent tidiness in keeping campsites orderly—"Better to use every minute enjoying the nature of the bush and surf beaches that abound in the park," was Nev's philosophy.

The more difficult the terrain in reaching our target, of course, meant that we were less likely to have other people around. So there were never crowds. So everything was more natural.

Only the fittest kids would go on these trips, and Laurie, Lynie, and other close mates would make up the complement. Even on some occasions, Middy, the very fat one, would make the special effort. It must have been painful for him with some of the really tough terrain we travelled—two hours or more of hiking from the train to the edge of the mountain of Nev's favourite beach, North Era, yet he never complained.

North Era was a small, pristine beach at the foot of a six hundred foot steep drop and had a freshwater stream flowing to it. The return journey was tough on all, particularly Middy, because our packs were heavy and terrain was rough.

Everything had to be carried on our backs—every scrap of food we would need, for instance, from Friday evening when we set out, to mid-afternoon Sunday when we must leave in order to reach home by a time satisfactory to parents. And our bedding, sun-screens and ointments, and between every two kids, for we slept in pairs, a pup tent. A sturdy trench-digger, too, had to be toted, not so much to dig run-offs around the tent when rain threatened, as to bury every bit of evidence before leaving so the site was left as pristine as we'd found it.

Whilst there were few rules other than those of 'safety and common sense,' as Nev called them, there was one important and significant condition. Every kid had to bring writing materials to write either prose, or poetry, or even music, depicting what we sensed in being part of such unspoiled nature. What we wrote had to be handed in within a month of getting home, to our English teacher if prose or poetry, language teacher if we chose to write in the foreign language we studied, or to Neville if it be music. If we didn't hand these in on time, we weren't eligible for more trips. A pretty neat way of sorting out the wheat among us from the chaff, Nev insisted. And me wanting to take English honours when my final year came, I got to find this a great sort of homework for writing essays.

So you might imagine how hefty were our backpacks. And we all had our share of things that would be needed by all, like kerosene lamps because we couldn't buy torch batteries during the war, fuel for them, tomahawks, and first aid gear. Nev never told us what foods to bring. Part of our learning was to make do with whatever was pooled. I would sometimes take potatoes and sausages, other times a pumpkin and fruit; some kids would take flour and stuff to make pancakes or damper. Sometimes we found we'd have to nearly starve, so we regulars quickly realised the need to do some bloody planning so we didn't end up with too much of too few—another lesson we were left to sort out among ourselves.

And we learned to live naked on these camps. North Era beach was so remote because of the difficulty getting there it was recognised as a nude bathing beach—if nudity appealed. I was one who at first never would, but after my Hornsby experience it wasn't so difficult, and I found surfing an infinitely more enjoyable sport to tackle when naked like the Abos.

Nev insisted on common-sense safety and told scatterbrained kids who took risks that they were off his list from ever coming again. And he kept reminding us of this list. It was even publicised at school that this kid or that kid had been blackballed from camping trips for not heeding cautions—so doors were really closed. There was no coming back. So we took advice seriously. And every kid learned after his first camp how bloody painful it was getting his pack up the mountain if he'd been careless enough to let his back or shoulders get even a little bit sunburned.

The North Era sandhills gave clear evidence that the beach had long been the local Aborigines' favourite. Huge areas of the sandhills had been middens—that is, densely covered with the weathered remains of eaten shellfish. Nev would never let us disturb these. "This area was obviously of spiritual importance to them," he would tell us—and often we would spend mealtimes and after talking about what Abo lore we collectively knew. And learning more. It all proved that they had pretty meaningful sorts of rituals. The size of the middens was testimony to that.

~ * ~

Mum and Pop were pretty good when it came to these sorts of things. Mum always had been. I'd learned to save up my pocket money against things I knew would arise either in the short or long term, and I seldom had to ask her for help. She would never refuse it but every time made me realise it was only a loan and that I'd have to let other things go in the longer term until I'd paid her back. And she made sure Pop didn't give me handouts, although I noticed that after she married, I got small increases in my pocket money more often. And I still had to work, no matter how much extra homework I got—and pay Mum something out of what I earned. That was for my keep when at home.

But I had Brisbane in mind again.

"Do you reckon Reecy would be up to having me again if I could afford my train fare?"

Mum told me she'd have to think about it.

Now what would she have to think about other than to ring Reecy and ask? But why couldn't she say that if that were the case? So next morning I tried another tack.

"What do you think about me writing to Reecy and asking her if I can come again after Christmas?"

Mum smiled, and Pop looked at her over the top of his glasses. I reckoned she had said something to him about it during the night, and there was some question in her mind over something—something not yet resolved.

Mum gave a second quick glance at Pop before answering.

"Yes, if you like. But there might be a problem."

"What's that?"

"Brisbane is not a safe place these days. There have been many fights in city streets at night, sometimes to riot stage. Even murders. It was in the papers not so long ago. Pop saw it and showed me."

I had seen nothing of this in the papers. Surely they would have been headlines, and I'd seen nothing. And I looked at the headlines every day.

"Riots over what? I saw nowt in any headlines."

"It wasn't in any headlines. You know they don't make headlines out of news that might shatter home morale, unless the sinking of a big ship or other. It was in a Sunday documentary. Pop always reads those."

"What sort of riots?"

Mum waved her hand at Pop, a sort of "Over to you, mate," gesture.

Pop took his specs off and looked me straight in the eye.

"Aussie soldiers and American soldiers get into heated arguments—"

"But we're friends—sort of all on the same side?"

Pop held up a hand as much as to say, *Let me finish.*

I shut up and sat back, waiting.

"Aussie servicemen get only six shillings a day by way of wages. The rest of their pay is put away in a reserve for two reasons. Firstly, the country needs cash to pay the costs of the war. Secondly, the saved money goes to the soldier's next of kin if he is killed, or will be given the soldier at the end of the war. There are many who would otherwise spend it all when on leave, on grog and women. Yanks receive pretty well all of their pay in cash. This means that when on leave, and Brisbane is the chief R-and-R destination for all South Pacific servicemen, Americans have money to spend on girls, and Aussies don't. This is causing problems. Aussies on leave cannot take girls dancing and drinking, and Yanks can. So on the streets late at night, the worse for liquor, Yanks with girls on their arms are targeted by Aussies, and fighting gets serious. It's not only the GIs and Aussies that get killed—sometimes, so are the girls."

When he sat back, Mum added her summing-up. "So Brisbane is not safe at night—and not only in the city. Do you remember that big vacant allotment opposite Reecy's shop where they used to raise the Big Top for the circus? Well that's now a military camp for American soldiers. Reecy told me in a letter only a few weeks ago that hand-grenades get lobbed into that camp, and many get killed or injured. So the killing is not confined to the city, but right on Reecy's doorstep."

Then Mum sat back.

Gee. What a terrible bloody war when even friends start killing each other.

But I still wanted to go. I had nearly enough savings already put away—half in my hidey-hole in Pop's garage and half in the money box in my low-boy.

"And another thing, boy..." Mum added. Whenever she called me 'boy' I knew she wanted a favour—a sort of 'do this or there will be hell to pay' sort of 'favour.'

"...That air raid shelter in the back yard. It's been full of water ever since you built it, and Pop, who knows things about drainage, says it will never empty because there's always seepage on this hill. It needs to be filled in. I was saving that up for your holidays. But if you want to go away, I'd like it done before you go. It's dangerous like it is. And I'm sure poor Millie downstairs thinks it an eyesore every time she comes onto her back veranda."

Mrs. Rowling downstairs had always been 'poor Millie' to Mum, since her husband got blown up.

"All right," I said, nodding. "I'll get to it. I'll get Laurie to come and help. I helped him dig a new rose garden for his mum. That was a favour she asked of him, so he owes me."

And Mum nodded. "But yes, you could write to Reecy. But I want to see what she says in her answer."

~ * ~

I was really getting toey about my swimming.

Freestyle was my *forte*, a French word I'd hijacked into my vocabulary. None of the two, four, or eight hundred metres stuff, however, because I was a sprinter—a hundred metres. The State High-School Swimming Carnival was coming up end of January, just a week before the new school year started.

Pop was keen to see me do well so gave me an early Christmas present: a week-long training session at the North Sydney Olympic Pool.

Gee, what an experience! I got down to the basics of training under an old codger that used to be an Olympic whiz, and he told me straight up that the object of the training session was to minimise the number of seconds my hundred metres took. It got right down to even every 'fraction' of a second being important, particularly with the breathing, not to mention the art of the turn at fifty metres. Or the dive. Or how I 'paddled' my feet.

He watched me do several lengths. "Don't try for speed, today" he told me, "until I've had a look at how you feel comfortable with your strokes. We'll work up to speed tomorrow. Today I want to see what you do in your natural rhythm."

He worked with me almost non-stop every day for a week, and yes, he did suggest changes but not as many as I expected. I had always kept my head low, breathing out while still underwater and on my fourth stoke breathing in under my left armpit as the arm came over. He changed none of that but worked on my paddle and the shape of my hands as I 'pushed.' Then we spent a whole day on the dive and two on the turn.

Wow! I was starting to feel toey about the High School Carnival come end of January—just a month away.

But I wanted to go to Brisbane in between Christmas and then.

~ * ~

By Christmas it was clear the Aussies had begun getting the better of the jungle war. We retook Wau, the last big New Guinea town that the Japanese had captured in their drive south. Was this the beginning of the Jap retreat from our doorstep that we'd all been hoping for?

The Americans were saying that since winning their Battle of Midway, things had been working well in pushing the Japanese back. In the Near-North Pacific, the Gilbert, Mariana, and Caroline Islands had been wrested from them. Warning was now being given to the Philippines that they were next on the US list of territories to be freed. Carrier-based aircraft were now bombing Japanese bases there. In the Southwest Pacific, US marines had begun their reclamation war when landing on Guadalcanal, pretty damned close to Australia, on my father's birthday...

...he's been dead these two years now, so might he have been up there, somehow seeing this happen on such an auspicious day?

The Yanks then worked their way through the Solomon Islands and Bougainville. The Japanese were defending with suicidal frenzy. They knew that if that island fell to the Allies, there were airfields that could be used to attack New Britain and New Ireland, last Japanese defences before the Philippines. With Japan now down to its last aircraft carrier, they were finding it difficult to defend territory so far from home.

Oh how war was changing!

It was becoming how far aircraft could fly that was now deciding the shape of war.

I turned up the First World War in my school history books, and only some thirty years ago the stumbling blocks had been hills and rivers. Then it was a matter of terrain—how tanks and troops could cope with obstacles. Now it was how superior was air power. Naval war had changed in that battleships with the greatest firepower then reigned supreme, whilst now it was aircraft carriers that decided strength.

Gee, I reckoned, how the Japanese must be kicking themselves that when attacking Pearl Harbour, the three US aircraft carriers were out at sea on exercises. Jap successes were destroying US battleships. The difference was to prove bitterly ironic as the war progressed. Only too late did Japan realise how remiss they had been in winning against battleships but missing out on the aircraft carriers.

Today, both sides were realising that irony.

Oh what a wonderful war this was turning out to be!

Twelve

Mum and Pop came to see me off.

We had had a quiet but happy Christmas at the home of one of Pop's daughters, and now I was off to Brisbane. I was made to promise that I would take Reecy's advice on when and where I could go out unsupervised. *If necessary,* Reecy had written, *I will send Edgar out with Kevvy.*

And I hated Kevvy even more than Kev.

I was delivered up to the only matronly sort of lady in my compartment on the train. In fact, apart from a floozy who even I could see would leave me to wolves if she saw a handsome GI, for instance, she was the only lady. All the rest were Aussie servicemen on leave.

She looked like I reckoned Old Crusty's wife would have looked.

"Is Brisbane your home, dear?" she asked as the train pulled out.

"No, but it used to be."

"Oh, is Sydney your home, then?"

"It was before I moved to Brisbane."

She seemed confused, but to me it was perfectly clear.

"Oh dear. Well, where is your home now?"

"Where the heart is," I told her. "And that's with the mother you just met."

And oh, my very dear! Had I ever won her heart so quickly! I could read it in her very face. I even heard sniggers from the guys sitting around. I felt like I was on a stage.

She pursed her lips just like Crusty's wife would have done.

"I think I can understand that." But then she followed with a real *faux pas*—another French expression I'd saved up for use in appropriate moments. "...I can't imagine anybody ever really feeling at home in Sydney."

The entire compartment fell silent...

Then she made the greatest *faux pas* of all. "All Melbourne people realise what an awkward place is Sydney."

The sniggers erupted into animated snarls. Here was a Snotty-Nose among us.

Wow! Has she ever declared her own war!

Weren't all these guys leaving Sydney on their way to Queensland? Even by my modest standards, it was clear they were all bloody banana-benders. The further north one got in this country, I knew, the less was thought of southerners—and the further south that southerners came from, the worse for them! And Melbourne was as far south as you could get, except for Tassie-types; and few would ever admit to being that... except, maybe, I thought on recollection, Merle and Ashe; and certainly my Mum; and Gran—oh, and also of course, Great uncle Fred who gave me his bike. But then too, I cogitated, looking for excuses, all of them, during their lives had bypassed Melbourne when moving north.

Awkward? What does she mean by that, I wonder? But at least she's noticed the snorts and realises the tenuous situation she's let herself in for. And we have some fifteen to twenty hours, yet, for all to get along well together.

She shut her mouth for the entire rest of the journey, and I had made many mates.

I settled back to start summing up all the reasons why I liked train travel. Trains had their own language. Their clickety-clack left no question in one's mind; it was a unique language that spelled out things like contentment, relaxation, and timelessness. I found listening to it far more enjoyable than listening to the Snotty-Nose, for instance. It was also a language that one didn't tire of, no matter how incessant.

And come morning, after having chosen, armed with past experience, to grab a card table from the rack at the end of each carriage, a solid board that would easily take my weight, to use as a bed in the corridor. I was cute enough... ah, memories of Amanda again, which brought on more trembles, of course... to clean my teeth in the washroom before its floor, too, became everybody's bed-space, and settled down to sleep. I was beginning to feel quite the experienced traveller.

Breakfast was the apple and banana that Mum had furnished me with. I followed orders and saved the Vegemite sandwiches for lunch. I knew none would go to waste, for most of the soldiers had brought nothing more with them than bottles of beer.

I didn't pass a word with the Melbourne Matron all the rest of the journey. I satisfied myself with scudding views of mountains and valleys, far more pleasing to the eye than the pert set of her mouth.

I had my scout whistle hanging on a lanyard around my neck. Mum had insisted I wear it to blow loudly and persistently on if any strange man on the train should force his way into the toilet behind me and lock the door. She spent considerable time over that warning. *Strange, what some women contemplate on,* I remember thinking.

Had Amanda Brixton been aboard, however, and again told me how cute I was, I certainly wouldn't have been blowing my whistle if she were to force me into a toilet and lock the door!

~ * ~

Wow. The big 'vacant' allotment across the road from Reecy's shop certainly was vacant no longer. A veritable city of prefab huts had been built to house US troops of all kinds, on rest and recreation leave. And Reecy was making a fortune out of them.

"They simply don't understand our money," she told me. "Pounds, shillings, and pence are like a foreign language to them. Firstly they've no way of mentally calculating what thirty-two and sixpence-ha'penny means in their dollars and cents, so they just spread out a pile of notes on the counter and trust me to take what I need. Then they trust me to give them the correct change. I never take them down, of course. Once any catches me out on being dishonest, that would be like I've killed the golden goose or whatever that saying is."

But then she blotted her copybook somewhat. "But I don't mind overcharging them. They're so convinced about this being a cheaper country than their own, that I add twenty percent on what I charge local people, and the Yanks still think things are cheap."

And she gave me a gorgeous wink as she said that. And I'd never tell on her, of course.

Pop told me that he'd read how Americans disliked being called Yanks. Well, some Americans, that is. It seemed only the people from the north of the country were Yankees, and those from the south were simply called Southerners. Well, all that was just too difficult to contemplate when talking about Americans collectively. Australians were called Aussies whether we came from Queensland or Tassie—even if from Western Australia, and that was so far from anywhere that I'd never even met one. But they were still Aussies. And Germans were all Krauts, and Japanese all Japs or Nips, so to try and sift different nicknames for Americans depending on where they lived, I reckoned was just too hard. And so it was, for all Aussies, easy to simply refer to all Americans, as 'Yanks.'

However, back to Reecy...

On my second night, it was Reecy's bridge night with crony friends, and she'd shut up shop early. Edgar and I shared a wired-in veranda as bedroom. It ran the length of the house against one of the side streets. His bed was one end and mine the other, and we took the opportunity of talking on things that weren't for Reecy's ears. It was clear they hadn't lived as man and wife for many a year, and Edgar confirmed that Reecy kept the door of her bedroom on the other side of the house padlocked.

"That's to keep me out, while she's out," Edgar told me, "and she also locks it from the inside when she's in—and that's also to keep me out." He giggled.

"She keeps money in there," he went on. "She don't trust banks any more'n she trusts me. 'If the bank fails because of the war, I'd lose everything,' is her argument. Never calls us 'we,' she don't, lad; it's always her *or* me. We share absolutely nowt any more—except maybe Pete, our son. He's up in the Owen Stanley's now, pushin' back the bloody Nips. 'My' son she always calls him, as if she don't even want to admit to her bloody self that I'm the boy's bloody father."

'Poor Edgar' I recalled thinking of him on my last visit—*and here it is two years later, and nowt is changed. He's still a lodger in his own house.*

~ * ~

Next day we heard over the radio that an American submarine was berthed in the Brisbane River and open for school visits. I was no longer a student in Queensland, of course, but I was keen to see a submarine close up even if not allowed aboard. I took the tram to Eagle street, wondering that if I were to show my school pass for the North Sydney pool where I was learning to swim properly, they might let me aboard, when... Wow! How lucky could a person get? When I arrived, there was a class of ten-year-olds from Windsor State, with who in charge? Talk about coincidence—it was Mrs. Allison!

I bounced up to her, and she recognised me straight off. "Oh, how you've grown," she greeted me, and she seemed happy at seeing me again. I told her why I was on holidays and why I had come to see the submarine.

"Just stay by me," she said. And when her class's turn came, no one questioned that I might look a tad old to be in the same class as the other kids. Maybe that I was right beside the teacher was proof enough that I wasn't a spy trying to get aboard, or something.

I told Mrs. Allison about my experience the night the Japanese subs came into Sydney Harbour.

"Oh, I remember when you addressed the class after your trip to Sydney by motor car. Will you have time before going home to come to school and tell these children about that night in Sydney Harbour? Nothing like that has ever happened here, of course. It might help them understand more about the war. Especially after they've been on a submarine."

I gave her Reecy's telephone number, and she promised to check a convenient date and then call me. We agreed that I would await the call on Thursday morning during 'play-lunch' time.

We were told by the captain that modern submarines had improved since the war started, that they could now carry more torpedoes, stay submerged longer, and travel faster under water. Then we were led below.

Oh, oh... All I could feel once cramped into such confined spaces was a need to get out. But I held my breath for long periods because I wanted to see an actual torpedo. Having done that, I straight away told Mrs. Allison I was going up—"If I don't, I'll panic," I told her. She explained later that there are many people in the world who 'can't abide enclosed space.' "It's called claustrophobia." Well! That was a nasty-sounding disease, all right, and I didn't even know I had it. I asked Ego if he'd known that, but he didn't even bother to answer.

I have ever since, however, had only the greatest admiration for the bravery of submarine crews—Australian, American, German, or Japanese. Every one, I reckoned, was a hero. From that day on, every news item mentioning submarines renewed that sense of respect.

But I'd not only seen a real torpedo, I touched it.

~ * ~

Next day over breakfast, Reecy and I talked about what programme I had set myself. And this was all in front of poor Edgar, just as if he weren't even there.

"Other than finding out when I'm to go to Windsor State, I've no fixed times."

"How's your mental arithmetic?"

The intriguing question surprised me.

"Not too bad. Old Mousy, my Maths Master, tells me I should think about sitting for honours in Maths-1, come fifth-year. And it has an 'oral section,' which I assume is mental maths. Why?"

"It's just that first thing of a morning, the shop is so busy, I get run off my feet. The Yanks have smoked their last cigarette during the night, or drunk their last bottle of soda, or got into a scrap and want aspirin or cold cuts of meat to put on black eyes. It would be great if you could help me—for just that first hour each morning."

"Do you still have prices marked on shelves and cupboards?"

"Yes. But now in small print that can't be read from across the counter. And you've got to be able to quickly add twenty percent to every price that doesn't yet have the higher price also marked. I haven't had time yet to do everything."

She led me along, showing me where some products already had the up-charge marked and some not.

"Well, how do you get on when you've got Aussies in the shop at the same time? Wouldn't some locals know your true prices?"

"By now they know how big the Yankee queues are, first thing, so most wait an hour except in emergencies. But it doesn't matter if they hear—it's on all the news broadcasts that Yanks are being ripped off everywhere they have to spend money."

I told her I reckoned I could do the sums easily enough. It was then agreed that 'near enough' was 'good enough.'

"But what if you're not here, or are busy with someone or something, if I have a price problem?"

"I'll be here while you're in the shop, just in case someone wants to argue…"

I smiled inside. I could already see even the toughest Marine who would invade a beach under heavy flak from the Japs and never flinch shuddering in his boots if fronted by Reecy with hands-a-hip. He'd surely surrender, like poor Edgar.

So I did help out for that hour each morning, and it was another new experience. Serving the first several guys was a bit traumatic, but all seemed matey and happy about getting fleeced—just like Reecy said. And she seemed happy the way I handled her money. She had little time to watch me anyway, I reckon. And all the guys liked her. She laughed with them, told them despite the crush how she could help all of them if they needed a motherly cuddle any time. "I could still teach the most experienced of you boys a few tricks," she would joke as she stole their money. And they all loved that.

It would be some of these very guys, my mind pondered, who would get into street-brawls with Diggers at night. I'd thought it was only in the cities, but no.

"On any street anywhere in Brisbane, wherever it's dark, which are most places, what with the lighting restrictions," Reecy and Edgar told me.

And yes, all streets were pretty dark. Even the entire accommodation section behind the shop had every window not only taped against flying glass but covered with light-barrier paper. And streetlights were on only at dangerous intersections and then only at a dim wattage.

Both Reecy and Edgar told me I must not venture out at night.

"I promised your mother that I'd report you to her if you disobeyed Edgar and me on this," she then told me. Then she put me right on the spot. "And I will lose respect for you if you make me keep that promise."

So I was grounded at night. Gee, fancy people being too afraid to go out in their own hometown!

~ * ~

The holiday couldn't be a long one. I'd had too many things on the go at home to be able to come for more than ten days all told, what with a two-night camp to North Era and me wanting to give an entire week to practising for the swimming carnival. And there was Gran's shopping every Wednesday. I'd deputised a neighbour's kid to do it while I was in Brissie.

I got my phone call from Mrs Allison.

"Is tomorrow all right?"

"Yes. But I'm helping my aunt at her shop first thing each morning. If I caught a tram at say ten, and it's only a few stops, would that be all right?"

We agreed on my arriving around eleven so I could give my talk before lunchtime.

But oh what a surprise when I stepped off the tram!

The entire huge playground, for a hundred yards in all directions around the swimming pool, was built up with the same sort of prefabs as opposite Reecy's. Here too, the American flag fluttered on a masthead. It too had been made over as a camp for US servicemen, including the swimming pool. I estimated the two camps, within a mile of each other, would accommodate several thousand men.

And my talk went off fine. The kids were the same ones I was with in the submarine. On the blackboard I drew a rough map of the appropriate part of Sydney Harbour to show them where was the naval base, the house where I slept, and where each of the two submarines were found—that which was tangled in the boom to blow itself up and that which was sunk in Taylor Bay.

And, "No," I told them at question time, "the third submarine that was sighted at one stage on the surface has never been found. We can only guess that it sank in a deep part of the harbour after being hit by depth charges."

They thoroughly enjoyed the recounting, and Mrs. Allison was happy.

When the lunch bell sounded, I joined the kids at the tuck-shop over the road, where I had the old pie and peas—more expensive than I remembered, yet still with free splashes of Worcestershire sauce from a bottle by the door. My stomach also enjoyed the memory.

I helped Reecy in the shop again through the afternoon, which certainly wasn't like the morning rush hour.

"They'll all be sleeping," said Reecy, "so they can go out tonight until the early hours or even until dawn. They get rotten drunk every night. You wait until you see them tomorrow. Some still won't be able to walk straight. They're the ones most likely to slap a pound note on the counter for a six and sixpenny purchase and tell me to keep the change!"

It all sounded just the same sort of scenario I'd pictured of the Aussie troops I met on the train, spending their time on leave—only with family.

After dinner, and having told Edgar to do the washing up on his own if I were not back in time, Reecy took me into her bedroom and locked the door behind us.

She had already brought in the till drawer and left it on the bed.

"You can help me count the takings," she told me.

"Well," she said when finished, "take twenty pounds off that for the change float I leave in it every night, and you can work out in your head what we made when I tell you that my estimate of what passed *out* over the counter in way of goods would have been worth little more than half of what came *in*, with change given."

"Whew!" I breathed noisily. "I wish I had a business like this."

"It's pure luck, you know, them building that place over the road and that this is the only general store without walking all the way up to Kedron Road then two blocks past the park."

And then I got an even bigger surprise.

"I can't lift all the mattress alone, and I need to tidy up the money piles while I have you to help. So let's move the mattress up against the wall."

And we did that.

My eyes boggled. I had never seen so much money. There were bundles of twenty-pound notes, tenners and fivers galore, with countless singles and lots of ten bobs of course—and even many US notes in all sorts of denominations.

"You see, the guys who are here now will be gone in a week, and a new lot will arrive. Every one of them wants to give me US money as tips."

Oh, you old rogue, I couldn't help but feel. Yet, as she had said, every guy left absolutely happy that he'd got his money's worth.

I helped her arrange the notes in some sort of order, then to lift the mattress back.

"She was naughty, yes," I told Mum when I got home, "but as she said, everybody was doing it, and the Yanks were happy."

"Our dear Reecy is a rich lady, I know. But one with a heart of gold as you must also know. Although poor Edgar mightn't agree with us."

Thirteen

And so back to Sydney.

Worst part of this trip was getting burning sparks in my eyes. There was no coal now. All coal went into the manufacture of metal for armaments. Trains had to run on wood, which meant lots of sparks, lots of bushfires, and the risk of careless passengers getting sparks in their eyes. I had raised the window because one larrikin in the compartment let off a most awful fart. I stuck my head out in a desperate attempt to get fresher air into my lungs.

I had become a dab at asking for a window seat on long-haul journeys. Things had got better organised by now, and one could again book seats. If it were a man at the ticket window—unusual in days when most men were off to war, but if say he had a wooden leg or doubly-thick bi-focals—I would tell him right off that my dad was somewhere on the Kokoda Trail, then hit him between the eyes with a request for a window seat. If it were a woman I'd tell her how much she looked like my mum, who I was on my way to visit because she was sick with worry about my dad being in the war. Soon as I saw a tear spring to her eye, I knew I had my window seat. They were such clever lies—all so convincingly plausible. White lies were normal those days; the government set the examples, which made near everything legitimate.

And the journey was never boring. During daylight hours, the countryside seemed so vast, a million miles from anywhere else and all so lavishly green. And I was, as well, a great people-studier. One can never get bored when there are people to watch. And in a crowd corralled together, like in a train, it becomes easy to laugh at little things and crack jokes, especially when most were soldiers or seamen on leave, when they seemed to chuck caution and common sense out the window.

But my eyes were really burned, and I was in awful pain. One bright guy ran along the corridor asking if anyone was a medic. Another poured water from a drinking flask into a handkerchief and had me lean back while he sponged out the offending ash. The burning sensation was quickly got rid of, but the flesh around one iris had been burned, and that remained sore. A medical corps guy arrived and had a cream to ease the pain.

"It's not the best, but the best I've got," he told me. "The guard says we're but twenty minutes of Grafton. He'll hold the train until I can get a tube of something more appropriate."

Everyone was attentive. I was very lucky about that. It proved that when there was real trouble, people would always put themselves out. But they didn't have to hold the train. The guard brought a first aid kit, and it had bandages and things, also an ointment the doctor was happy with. So while I didn't look it, what with half my head bandaged, I felt pretty much all right by morning when we made Sydney.

I got the bandage off at Hornsby, however, from where North Shore passengers transferred to local trains before the interstater continued on the loop to enter Sydney from the south. For North Shore residents, the trip was that way shortened by an hour. I got the bandages off in the gents' washroom so Mum wouldn't have a heart attack on seeing me.

And the eye was soon comfortable again; fortunate indeed, I reckoned, in that as soon as tomorrow, I needed to be in the pool again.

And an exciting event of the war also happened next day. We got to hear about it, of course, at breakfast.

The Americans had made a second landing on the Italian mainland. The first, a mixed contingent of Allied armies, including some Aussies, had got bogged down south of Naples. The German *Wehrmacht* had mounted a stronger defence than Italians habitually did. However, from the new site at Anzio, the Americans were able to drive south to link up with the southern army, trapping the Germans on the coast. Many prisoners were taken. So that was good news to come home to.

And there was a message for me from Dad's brother, Uncle Harold.

"He wants to talk with you about your future," Mum said. "He wants you to phone him."

Harold had a successful business and was the rich one of our family. He'd told me before that with my dad dying, he wanted to do for me what he thought his young brother would expect of him. He wanted me to come to his office in the city and talk with him. I told him about my training for the Carnival, and he was excited that I was doing so well with my swimming. He asked me dates and did I yet know what date and time were my heats. I didn't yet know, but I told him I would try to find out.

"Well, I want to talk with you this week, son. What time does your training finish each day?"

"It's up to me, but I really do want to spend as many hours at it as I can."

We arranged I would arrive at his office before five the next afternoon.

He wanted me to change schools.

'Shore', the popular name for the North Sydney Church of England Grammar School, a celebrated GPS—a Great Public School, which I always thought a misnomer when it wasn't public as in government-owned as it was privately owned—was coincidentally located only a few hundred yards from North-Tech, a government school.

"I will pay your fees, lad," he told me. "I went to that school, and your Uncle Ken..."

'Uncle' Ken was ostensibly a nephew of Harold. Whilst Harold considered Ken a 'surrogate son,' family rumour had it that Ken was likely the illegitimate son of Harold and his brother Ted's wife! But that could never be mentioned, of course.

Ken had also been schooled at Shore.

"And so would your father have been, lad, had he, like you, not been forced into a lesser school because of a World War. So Shore is traditionally the Richardson family's school. It has turned out highly qualified men, lad, including several prime ministers."

I knew Shore was a good school. Some Shore kids played in the Scout Rugby competition on Sundays, and many had become friends. But I was so happy at North-Tech. I was training to be one of the country's great architects and didn't want the interruption of leaving all that to move to Shore. And many of my best mates were at North-Tech. And the North Era Camping trips—I loved those. The swimming wasn't a problem, because training was available in both.

I told Uncle, "No," that I didn't want to change schools halfway through my five senior years.

"I do my Intermediate this year, Uncle. And I'm being encouraged to sit for honours in three subjects for my Leaving in forty-six. I've got my swimming organised to fit it in with Scout activities—in fact I've set my goal at becoming a King's Scout before I'm seventeen when I have to move up to Rovers. And that's January '46. So I've limited time to achieve all that. And when swimming season finishes, rugby starts, and I play that every Sunday. Shore boys in that comp say Shore makes it awkward for them because the Scout Rugby programme clashes with Shore's."

I could tell he felt like he was fighting a losing battle, for he quickly backed off offering alternate reasons.

"If I ask Ken to talk with you on this, would you do that? He has sons of his own now, and he already has them booked into Shore. Ken was there a lot more recently than me, of course so I'd like you to hear whatever he has to say. Eh, lad?"

I had nothing to lose. I liked Ken. He was Harold's second in command in the business, and if Harold threw this challenge at him, he would feel doubly pressed to convince me. But so long as I was careful not to make decisions on the spot, I would see what Ken had to say.

~ * ~

Was my sister a secret agent for the Yanks?

It became quite a question in my mind.

She finished high school before Christmas and was ready to join the workforce. I arrived back from Brisbane to discover she already had a job.

She was working for the American War Office. It rented an entire eight-floor building in York Street. She told me she couldn't tell me the real name of the department, nor the floor she was on. I was interested in that because I knew it as a tall building.

"I'm doing bookkeeping, and that's all I can tell you. I'm sworn to secrecy because of the war."

Well! That didn't satisfy me one little bit. I knew she had studied bookkeeping at school, but there was a principle involved.

I am her brother, for God's sake, I exclaimed to Ego. *This is Australia. I reject any notion that any American has a right to insist my sister keep secrets from her own brother. Who do they think they are?*

But he advised me to cool down before I sprang a leak.

"What do I tell my friends when they ask where my sister works? How do I answer questions on what she does there?"

When I posed that to Val, she told me I should simply tell them I didn't know.

"Now you're asking me to lie to my friends?"

"It's not a lie when you really don't know. I'm just trying to make it easier for you. Every employee has promised not to tell anyone anything about what we do, or what anybody else does. That's surely a reasonable request in wartime."

"Do they pay you in dollars or real money?"

"In pounds, of course."

"Are you going to tell me how much?"

"No. You are still a child at school. I'm now working for a living, and it's a different sort of life."

"Your life is no different. You still live here, you still take the tram to the city, you still eat the same foods I do. It's the same sort of life."

"Then why so many questions?"

This seemed all so unreasonable. It was a war situation I couldn't be part of.

What if, I asked Ego, *she gets kidnapped by German or Jap spies—tortured, has unspeakable things done to her until she tells them everything?*

~ * ~

Come Easter, Neville Meal arranged an exacting trek for our group. By now we were highly experienced in bushwalking and camping. This was a four-night and five-day hike from Botany Bay and Port Hacking via the coast, along beaches and over the several rocky headlands that separates each, to North Era. The entire area, all National Park, was devoid of people other than intrepid hikers and campers. There was no halfway measure—once started it was either finish the goal or admit defeat and return all the way you had come— an entirely unacceptable option to any dedicated hiker.

"Except for the first day," Nev told us when detailing what we were committing to, "is the pure excitement of having as many spots to surf naked as there are to discover bubbling streams descending from the coastal heights, ideal for pitching camp."

Starting point was a ferry from Cronulla, most southerly of Sydney's score of suburban beaches, to Bundeena on Port Hacking's southern shore. By now we were all experienced bushmen and could eat well, not only from food brought with us but from what we could gather along the way—snakes and such. On that trip it was a goanna. At end of each day, Nev, having set daily goals, would detail what was in store for tomorrow.

"If we don't meet each day's goal," he pointed out, "it means we can't start that difficult climb up the range on the last day without having had an overnight rest."

And it was unthinkable, we four mates agreed, that we could ever let the situation arise that it become known at school that we hadn't met the criteria. Absolutely unthinkable! So each day, blisters or tummy upset or any other pain was forced into the bodily-secrets file until reaching our night's goal. Common sense then prevailed, and we would seek whatever help our supplies contained. This approach to team effort helped bind friendships even more tightly—as if we were in the war in New Guinea's jungles with all their uncomfortable challenges!

Nev promised that on our last day but one, at a particular little cove that he showed us on the army ordinance map he used for such hikes, we would have a new experience. But he would tell us no more than that.

"You particular four," he declared, "will enjoy it—I promise you."

So all through that day, we let him call the tunes on how long we could spend thrashing around naked in the surf before drying out, dressing, then helping each other into the harnesses of our heavy packs for the next several hours afoot.

When we reached the little cove, one without a regular 'cliff' to climb down to but a track that only someone in the know could find, someone like Neville who had, he now told us, used it many times, he called a halt.

"Leave your packs here. We are far enough off the beaten track that they won't be found for the hour our visit will take, and the hour to descend to the beach and return. But bring whatever food we have left. I've a bag here for that. We can take turns carrying it."

What a tease he could be, I couldn't help but feel. But he had me tingling with anticipation of what we could find down there. We were to bring all the food we had between us? With yet two nights to go? And leave our packs with our tents and things, here?

I felt like a kid on the night Santa was due.

We hung our packs in trees. Despite they contained no food, we still didn't want ground creatures gnawing their way in, in search of anything.

An old hermit lived on the beach. How old he was, was hard to tell because he had the sort of beard that he simply took to now and again, it was clear, with a pair of sheep shears and no mirror. It was obvious that Neville knew him well, and the old fellow made us welcome, despite he had nowt to offer. He was stark naked, and I've never seen a body so wrinkled and scarred. He had a sort of half-hut built in a cave off the tiny beach—built from driftwood and tree branches. We sat on rocks that were his only furniture except an old sea chest—yes, a real old sea chest right out of the *Treasure Island* movie. He'd been there some twenty years and never left. His diet was mostly snakes, or sea gulls that he stunned with a catapult.

"The war?" he asked when I asked how he learned about what was happening with it. "What war is that?"

He said it with a smile. He knew there was one, but nowt of what it was all about. Nor did he care—nor about anything else 'out there.' Nothing of the life we lived concerned him in the slightest. The authorities didn't know he was there. Even the park rangers kept mum about his existence, Nev later told us. Nev had us rummage through our sack of food to sort what we could do without for the rest of our journey. And oh my goodness...

When we looked at what we had that we could leave for him, then what we had reserved for ourselves, his share seemed so little. We looked at each other, then at Nev, but he said nothing, simply smiled and waited.

Laurie reached into our pack and took out another can of tomatoes, then passed the pack to me. I took out cheese and a can of corned beef. Bruce added a packet of biscuits, Bryan a small pumpkin. Bryan passed the pack to Nev, who looked inside. He handed over the two remaining cans of condensed milk.

"We can drink black tea for the next two days," he said. Then turned to the old man. "The can-opener still work?"

The old man nodded.

"Your spoon still all right, and your fork?"

The old man nodded again.

Nev reached into a pocket and handed him a toothbrush.

"Okay, boys, time to go. Watch your heads as you stand."

You have to envy a man like that, I reckoned, as well as suffer a perverse sort of anguish when wishing him, on parting, nowt but more lonely meditation.

We were all very quiet after resuming our trek.

It wasn't until over a more meagre dinner than we would otherwise have had, a fact referred to by none, that we talked about how we thought a man could live twenty years alone, with no goals, nor care about anything or anybody.

Neville smiled as he listened to what his charges felt about the experience.

Only then did he make a comment.

"He cares more conscientiously than any of you, or me, about preserving nature. He is on talking terms with entire wallaby families that visit him here. And I believe him when he tells me a family of porpoises also visits frequently and lets him surf with them."

~ * ~

Having slept on our yesterday's experience, we all woke feeling somehow renewed. Each found ourselves baring something of our inner selves as we surfed before breakfast and after it, packed, ready to make our way to North Era.

Was it something from that experience that caused us to begin releasing some of the secrets we'd each, up until now, been too reticent to share? Without prompting, we seemed to begin letting friends see into our private souls. On a hike such as this, just us five, four brotherhood mates and Neville, who we kept forgetting was five or six years older, we began bonding as one—for every minute of every hour still remaining. I suddenly realised we were sharing thoughts that we'd ever secreted, figuratively, in our nethermost bowels. We were now tossing into the ring for others to comment on doubts considered too confidential to unveil previously to these same friends—like how to approach girls, like the burdens of sexual ignorance, sorts of "Am I queer or what?" situations—questions we couldn't bring ourselves to discuss even with parents.

Neville never made comment unless invited, I noticed only after some time. He simply proved himself a good listener. Until invited...

"I'm just happy to hear boys at last realising a situation where they can toss these problems around. I don't see it my role to offer advice because I too harbour doubts. Everybody does. No man or woman can ever be close enough to your problem, Ric," he said, pointing his walking cane at me, "or yours," now pointing it at Laurie, then at others in turn,

Bryan Lyne and Bruce Rowles. "You boys are each other's friends, and I simply enjoy having created opportunity for you to open up with each other—those in whom you already have confidence. If I feel, however, that any of you have raised attitudes that several years of this experience have taught me are inappropriate, then I'll raise a question. Just don't ask me to give you answers. You've to search out your own. Sharing concerns with peers will help you do that."

Later we boys talked about that while washing dinner dishes in the surf.

"In the surf?" you might ask?

Well, on this occasion, yes. It was high summer, and the drought was severe, meaning there was little water in the creek. Nev insisted that instead of cleaning our dishes and cook-pots in the creek as usual, we take them over the sandhills to the surf.

"When water is so scarce," he'd tell us, "we need to save what little there is for the mountain's wallabies that come down to drink."

We decided how lucky we were to have a teacher like Neville. On the one hand, he always kept insisting we be conscious of the environment we were in. And he seemed to create opportunities, we discovered along the way, of being conscious of other people's personal problems that they seemed ever cautious about keeping in their background. Other masters at school seemed to ignore that, simply telling us what they reckoned we needed to know, not trying to make us aware of the importance of friends—the benefits of sharing life's difficulties...

It sort of encouraged us to seek solutions for such problems, rather than simply feeling hard done by them.

Fourteen

By April, the last Japanese was driven from New Guinea.

Wow! What a long and testing campaign that had been for our Diggers!

We were suddenly, after seldom seeing any photos in the papers when losing battles, getting lots of photos. The Owen Stanley Range was rough country. I by now considered myself something of a bushwalking authority, and the pictures we were getting illustrated hardships I'd never had to face. Valley walls there were vertical by comparison, and ridge trails so thick that before a man could take another step he must clear the space for it with a machete. Mates following would then widen the track to get supplies through. Local tribesmen were used as porters and stretcher-bearers, for it was often a long and tedious haul to where tent hospitals could be set up. And all the while, while battling the terrain, every man realised that deadly hails of gunfire could erupt from any direction.

But it was the Abos that really brought messages home to me—mystically, that is. Aboriginal tribesmen were brought in to help with communications.

The constant dampness of jungle, the incessant rain, and the fact that electric storms raged day and night in much of New Guinea's mountainous north, made radio contact between forward positions, back-up sources, and 'brass' unreliable in the extreme. And physical conditions made the use of 'runners' impossible.

No one knows how they do it, but Aussie Aborigines really do have extra-sensory powers when it comes to communicating. We kids growing up used to poo-hoo claims that Abos could 'point the ceremonial bone' at some miscreant or enemy, and sure enough, even though that guy wasn't within *Cooee* of the bone being pointed—even fifty miles away—he would quickly develop stomach pains and die. It was found that these guys could actually do it.

In Aussie history books, tales from the earliest white settlement told of Aboriginal prisoners locked in cells 'singing' themselves to death—literally singing a cant in their strange rituals, to be next morning found dead—with not a scratch or physical mark on them.

To this day nobody knows how they do it, but they can not only call on spirits to act for them from a distance but actually transmit messages to each other. After the war it was to come out that in the New Guinea campaign, we actually took Abos from the same tribe to the front lines. Some would go with the forward parties, and others stayed with the brass. Messages from their brethren could be delivered by mental telepathy. It worked!

How it worked, no white man, scientist, or magician has ever been able to fathom. Maybe we will never know. We know only that they can bloody do it!

Such 'bush-telegraph' really helped kick the Japs out of New Guinea before they could get to Rabaul. Only that far south was terrain open enough for airfields from which to bomb not just Darwin, but every Australian city, coal and copper mine, and steelworks, essential to the Allied war effort.

That's how close it bloody got!

~ * ~

Much was happening at the Scout Hall.

We weren't doing too well in the rugby comp but were 'scooping' the swimming pool. John Davies and yours truly were turning in great times, especially John. He went on to swim for Australia at the

London Olympics and then to win the only Aussie gold in Helsinki. So even back in Scouts I was in good company. John trained at Roseville baths, I trained at the North Sydney pool, and both began about this time, winning cups at school competitions. I was a sprinter—fast over a hundred metres. John's speciality was the two hundred metres breast-stroke. So at annual Scout Swimming Carnivals, where 'local' troops mounted mini-carnivals, First Chatswood was really on top. John and I both felt ten feet tall.

All that sort of slipped in, because what I want to really tell here is about the Roseville foreshore right by the very pool where John trained. It was our nearest 'undeveloped' reach of Sydney Harbour, and everyone in the world, so the ads were to reckon after the war, knows about Sydney Rock Oysters. In New York, for instance, even during the late 1940s, a half dozen were costing restaurant patrons a cool twenty dollars. But they didn't cost us kids a penny.

Those of us with pushbikes would pick up mates who didn't, and we'd scoot down to the Roseville reach on spare weekends, equipped with strong, sharp knives. I had at home under the stairs vice and emery wheel so I would sharpen all the knives and bring them, and also pliers. Another kid would bring empty jam cans, jam being packed in one-pound tin cans those days, and others would bring candles and matches. How many hours I spent over a two or three year period around this time of my life, slipping fresh oysters down my throat, I couldn't count. Come low-tide we would cut the candles low enough that they didn't blow out once stuck in the bottom of the jam-tins, then light them, and as many of us as had knives would scoop huge oysters off the rocks at low tide, grip them with pliers, hold them over the flame, and bingo! Within seconds the lid would snap open. We'd scoop the oyster from its grip on the inside of the shell, upend the shell on our lips, and let the oyster slide down our throats—dozen after dozen.

Wow! Did any kid ever have it so good?

The other big, exciting thing to become habit at the Scout Hall was dancing ...

We kids were getting to the age of appreciating the great music coming out of England and America, and some of us even had records.

Most families had gramophones, and lucky kids had portable ones, popular in army barracks and aboard ships. I had an old one because I bought it out of my earnings running deliveries for Mr. Frazer. It needed a new spring, but so long you stood over it winding as it played, it worked passably well. That was possibly why it was so cheap!

A lady and her husband who were good dancers would bring along a real good portable and lots of records to teach all kids who wanted to learn how to dance. All for free. Every scout with a sister was told to bring her along—if more than one, the more the merrier. Well, mine wouldn't be in it. She was too busy in off-hours doing voluntary work some evenings and weekends at the Services Social Club in Kings Cross, helping with cooking, making beds, and serving in the bar for men on leave from all Aussie services.

I didn't really mind my sister not being at the dances. That risked news of what I might be up to at times getting back to Mum and Pop. But a kid in my Curlew Patrol had an older sister...

The curlew is a bird I don't recall ever seeing but which spends its time wading in shallows eating worms and small crabs, all of which seemed to me a useless bloody pastime. I'd rather have had our patrol named Kookaburra for instance. The kooka was a smart bird—and useful. It would carry a surprisingly large snake up a tree to there smash its head in by beating it against a branch before eating it, then laugh its head off. The curlew did nothing clever. Of all the badges I studied for in Scouts, I never did go in for bird watching. Maybe I might have, if I'd been a Kooka instead of a Curlew.

Well, this kid, Barry Wellersley by name, a freckled runt who proved in scouting circles, in my opinion, as useless as a curlew, said he'd bring his sister along. And she wasn't bad. Girls to me at that stage were 'not bad' when a first-sight opinion indicated she 'could' have potential. She wasn't as freckled as her brother, nor Cilla Addams, and about as tall as Amanda Brixton, so all that somehow added up to 'possible potential.'

I knew she was happy to talk to me because Barry told me she'd slipped him a tray if he would introduce her to 'the dark-haired' bloke in his patrol who won the sprint at the swimming carnival her parents had to 'drag' her to.

So I knew that as far as she was concerned, I had elevation. I had remembered 'position of some elevation' described a guy in a movie Val and I had seen who had women flocking after him. I'd kept it in mind ready to use if ever getting so lucky. *And this could be that time*, I told Ego.

Since I was a kid, Mum had often whisked me around the floor when a waltz came on the wireless, and I'd done the barn dance often enough at weddings and things, but what I wanted to learn was the quickstep. Clark Gable would whisk Myrna Loy around, as would Fred Astaire with Ginger Rogers, to the sort of music Mum told me was a new thing called the quickstep. Those sorts of guys always got the girl they wanted, and they did really dashing dancing.

But while Peggy Wellersley looked all right at first sight, it was a case of, "But can she dance?" Not that I wanted to be a better dancer than her already, but I'd want her to have rhythm in her body like Mum told me I had. I wanted it to be a situation where we could learn together, that I wouldn't have to feel myself in a 'catch-up' situation.

"Can you dance?" I asked.

"A little bit."

Well, what did that tell me? She wouldn't have said, "Yes, I'm very good," even if she had been, of course, but 'a little bit' told me nothing. I'd just have to wait and see. I hoped they'd start with the waltz so I wouldn't look an absolute idiot.

"Barry said you came to the swimming carnival."

I knew this safe ground to start on. I already had a point on the board here.

"Yes, I saw you swim. You were very good."

"Thank you. I try hard. I train a lot."

"Barry says you have lots of badges, more than anybody else in the troop."

I nodded. "Yes, I like scouting. I hope to become a King Scout."

Ah Ric, you idiot! That's one too far! You shouldn't have said that. It's true enough, of course, but you shouldn't have introduced an *'if' situation. You had the bloody floor; now you've introduced a new level you've got to start trying to justify!* Why couldn't I have been satisfied with being on winning ground instead of introducing a 'maybe' situation?

Because you're stupid, as well as vain, Ego whispered.

Peggy was fifteen.

Careful, Ric! Don't fall into another trap. Don't ask her when her birthday is. I turned fifteen three months ago and I don't want her older than me. I'll have to just play this by ear until I can ask Barry about her birthday. Right now, though, I'd better change the subject.

"Do your parents dance?"

"They used to. My father's away in the war now. He's in the Air Force."

"Mine's dead. But I can remember Mum and Dad every Saturday night all dressed up for the Saturday night dances—Mum in long dress and gloves, Dad in tails and white gloves. They could do all the dances. I liked watching them Charleston. They were great at that."

"Can you Charleston?"

"Maybe it'd come to me if I heard the right music. But it's the quickstep I want to learn."

"Ooh, yes. Me, too."

Well at least here's a start!

"You like us to start partners?"

She nodded. Then giggled.

Ah! She's got dimples! That's a second 'potential' point.

~ * ~

By mid-year things were looking up everywhere. I would often try looking at life and couldn't help but see it as some sort of game— or sport—and when one started counting up, yes, there were enough wins on the board to make one realise that if you worked on things, there were rewards.

And the war was part of that.

In Europe, in the Pacific, and at the Scout Hall, things were suddenly now all going great.

The greatest armada of ships the world had ever seen sailed across the English Channel with British, American, Canadian, and Aussie troops. The Western Front had opened, and Germany had to withdraw troops from its Eastern Front. Oh, the dilemma the Germans must be feeling. If France fell to the Allies, Germany would be under attack on the ground as well as in the air, and already Allied bombers from England were lambasting German cities.

Also, the Russians would now find even weaker resistance on Germany's Eastern Front.

In the Pacific, Americans were pounding the Japs in the Solomon Islands and the New Britain Group. Pop reckoned America was keen to regain air bases within reach of Japan so they could not only begin destroying Japan's manufacturing bases, but paying them back for their sneaky attack on Pearl Harbour.

Our boys had found in New Guinea that Japs never surrendered. They reckoned surrender was worse than death, so they would fight to the bloody death.

Taking back all the Pacific nations, the East Indies, Philippines, and all the small island nations before getting airports close enough, therefore, was going to be a costly exercise.

Things were a lot easier at the Scout Hall, however. Dancing classes went well but not quickly enough for Peggy and me. They had decided we should start learning old time ballroom dancing first so it was things like the barn dance, Gypsy tap and Schottische, a sort of polka. But at least I could pull rank on young Barry, me by now being his patrol leader. I'd make him ride my bike to his home at the end of each dance night while Peggy and I walked, holding hands. He'd never get too far ahead but stop and wait until we caught up. It was pretty clear, I reckoned, that his mum had told him not to let Peggy and me out of his sight.

When we got to her home, however, Peggy would scoot Barry inside while we said goodnight. We couldn't do much because we knew Barry, even if not his mum also, would be watching from behind curtains. She would jump up to plant a kiss on my cheek but mostly her aim was never good. It usually caught me somewhere in the vicinity of my left ear. But then we'd giggle. Then I'd cycle home. One night, however, the little bugger Barry, as a joke, let all the air out of my front tyre. Peggy, on going inside could hear Barry giggling as he watched me, hands a-hip, staring at my tyre. She marched him out the front door, holding his ear. I made the little bugger go get his pump from the garage and pump my tyre up again.

~ * ~

It was mid-year, and winter, so there was no swimming and no training, just rugger. For my birthday, Mum and Pop had given me a pretty advanced sort of Spanish galleon to model from balsa. It had all the sails and pennants and things in coloured paper as part of the kit and twine for the rigging. I'd always enjoyed working with wood, and Dad had left me excellent tools, so now I dug this gift out from where I'd stashed it. Summers were not the time for doing indoor things—mine were too taken up with swim training and camping to fit in around my chemist deliveries after school and still doing Gran's shopping Wednesdays, and homework with this year being Intermediate before going into concentrated studies on chosen subjects next year. All summer, every year, I found pretty damn busy.

Over the mid-year months by now though, I was going less frequently to the footy with the Gordons, so I worked on the galleon while listening to war news on the wireless. I finished the ship in time for the August Scout Fair, and it won first prize for the handicraft division. So I was chuffed about that. It entitled me to another badge. I had so many badges by now that I couldn't fit any more on the sleeves of my scout-shirt. I had to start sewing them on the shirt itself. I had more badges than any other kid in the troop—and all other local troops in fact. Three more, and I could submit my application for King's Scout.

The war was going great if you didn't count the number of men being killed.

We now knew it unlikely that we would ever get bombed, and that helped morale a hell of a lot of course, but casualties mounted the more territory that had to be cleared of Japs.

The Allies in Europe had made a landing on the south coast of France, the quicker to open up yet another front to divide German forces that were soon so weakened that Paris was liberated not by Allied forces but French Resistance fighters. Oh, and were they ever taking it out on French people who had collaborated with the Germans, helped them during the occupation! And the same in Italy. Italian partisans dragged Mussolini out of prison and hung him and his mistress upside down by the ankles for the populace to make mockery of.

At the Scout Hall, we'd progressed to modern ballroom stuff, and Peggy and I got good at the quickstep. But I was having far less luck than Clark Gable or Fred Astaire when it came to personal things. Peggy was playing hard to get…

Or was it that she'd been told by her mother to keep me at arms' length?

And I lived with this quandary until one night, on walking her home, she led me around the side of her house where no one could see us from any window. There she leaned up to be kissed on the lips, so I squeezed her tight just like the heroes in the movies always did—before then trying a bit of my own subtlety. The kiss was nice, but as we pulled apart, I put a hand on her bosom, not tight, just anxious to see what she would do. But it wasn't at all what I expected.

She slapped my face and told me she never wanted to see me again.

Well! But what had I really done wrong? I was so sure that that was what would have been the hero's next move at the flicks, although they could never show it on screen. But it hadn't worked. Peggy never came to dance classes again, and Barry never said even a word to me about it. Maybe she never told him. But maybe she told her mother, so I reckoned I had better just write the whole thing off as a flick experience with a sad ending.

Pity though.

Fifteen

Belgium and Holland were liberated during September.

The Allies, now in a continuous line from the Mediterranean to the North Atlantic, were pushing relentlessly towards Germany.

On the Eastern Front, the Russians were pushing the Germans back through Poland.

Next we heard was that General MacArthur was fulfilling his promise of invading the Philippines. In a major naval battle off Leyte Island, the Aussie and American navies decimated what was left of the Japanese fleet.

I learned from the papers that the Japanese fleet was now in tatters, that the Allies were clearly, by now, masters of the entire Pacific—great news, all right.

Dislodging Japanese troops from every island in the Western Pacific, however, wouldn't be easy. Without a navy to pull troops out, Jap soldiers would only defend each island with more vigour—provided supplies were flown in. Yet I reckoned our generals would be keeping their eyes on that problem

I spent as many afternoons as I could training at the pool for the High Schools Swim Carnival. It would be at the North Sydney Pool, and during every training lap I tried to imagine it was not even a heat that I was swimming, but a final, so that I turn in best times. It was not only breathing, stroking and kicking I was practising of course, but diving and turning. I knew the body wasn't yet up to winning the school title because I was still swimming against kids two years older. But oh! If I could even get a place!

My job delivering for Mr. Frazer had been handed on to another because I was also swatting for my Intermediate. Then I had two years of concentrated study for the Leaving Certificate. It was in that final year that I wanted the title! Uncle Harold had already said that, starting next year, he would pay for special coaching in the subjects that in 1946 I wanted to sit for Honours.

So I had two really busy years coming up.

~ * ~

The swimming carnival was a disaster. I won my heats as expected, yet in the final with everyone rooting for me on the turn I took a gulp of water and, trying to cough it up before swallowing it, missed half a beat. There was no way I could catch up the inches I lost. I came in fourth. Bloody Hell! But John won his breaststroke, so at least come scout's night we had that to celebrate.

Everything was head down and tail up, as they say as I counted down days until end of November and first week of December.

I was still swatting for exams. I didn't know where the time went, because I just couldn't fit everything in. Even dance classes had gone by the board. And Nev had organised a North Era camp for our group for the weekend following the exams. *It's pretty true, sometimes,* I reckoned, *that you get the feeling that no matter hard you try to fit everything in, it's simply not good enough, like the watched pot that they say never boils—which is true enough in itself; although isn't it also true, that as soon as you take your eyes off it, it boils over?* You know what I mean.

Mum and Pop told me they were planning another visit to Katoomba.

"Just for a weekend," they said.

My mind raced a minute mile... A bloody break would do me good, too...

"Can I go stay with Alan?"

Suddenly, even a day there, so long as Amanda Brixton was free, flashed through my mind. *And as long as Alan wins a short straw!*

Oh! My mind raced another minute mile. *Yes, that's what I want.*

"I'll ring Alan and see if it's all right with the Addams," I said.

"If Val, then, can come with us, or go to Sue's again, we guess that's all right. A break from your studies would do you good. But only for one night."

The memory of Amanda Brixton calling me cute as she'd held my balls again had me horny. I sat down and crossed my legs. I had to get quickly to Val to see what she wanted to do.

But I rang Alan anyway.

"Yeah, that'll be great," Alan said. "Cilla will be pleased."

"I was hoping Amanda might be willing."

"If that's what you want, I'll organise it so I draw the straws."

"Ah! You're a real friend."

"Well, you have to do something towards it this time. You bring the condoms."

My pulsing heart missed a beat as up sprang a sense of horror. But I couldn't say, "No." We arranged that I'd train up on the Saturday morning and come back Sunday evening.

"So either Saturday afternoon or Sunday morning will be okay, whichever suits the Brixtons," I told him.

"Bring four condoms, and we can do both."

Ah! Again!

How to get the condoms? Buying four was no greater problem than buying two; the problem was, of course, going into a pharmacy and asking! If I'd still been working for Mr Frazer I could do it. Of an evening when the girls had left, he would usually wait until I was back from a delivery to watch the shop while he went for a piddle. Then I could simply put them in my pocket and give him the money, telling him I'd sold them to a randy Digger. And I didn't know a pharmacy that didn't have girls behind the counter. And what if there were different sizes?

I rang Alan again. He laughed but told me what to ask for.

"Just breeze in and ask same as if it's toothpaste. That makes girls so embarrassed they just want you out quickly in case you comment on their blushes."

That did little to satisfy my problem of course. So I asked Laurie.

"Do your own dirty work," was his answer. I knew he was miffed with me for having such luck on the last occasion—but in a good-natured sort of way. It was envy.

But I did the deed. I'd read somewhere that Aussies earned for themselves, when growing up, an inbuilt capacity for self-denial, and I reckoned that that was pretty well the situation I was in. So I did it like Alan suggested—waited until the shop was empty of any other customer and quite denied myself the agony of feeling embarrassed. And there were no blushes, nor any particular hurry. She simply counted out my change and didn't even bother to wrap them. I wondered later, however, if that was because I snatched them to plunge into a pocket the instant she laid them on the counter, in case somebody else came in.

And Amanda? Oh dear yes. I think I should do here, in respect of what happened that weekend, exactly as the censor did to incoming mail from servicemen—cut a great hole in the page so no secrets are divulged!

All I could think of as my Sunday evening train sped homewards... *Peggy Wellersley, eat your heart out!*

~ * ~

Having overcome an insatiable desire, once home, to strip my sister's pin-ups of Nelson Eddy from all over the laundry walls to replace them with Amanda Brixton pinups—overcome because I had no pinups other than mental ones—and having the flat to myself for the first time in my life, I decided not to swat. Instead I would let my exultation relax with a little light music from the wireless. I chanced on the *Glen Miller Hour*. Every Sunday night, the ABC put on an hour of popular music and tonight was Glen Miller, he whose wonderful stuff had me gliding around the Scout Hall floor with, in the early days, Peggy W, she whose full name was now wired out of my memory forever, and more latterly any other free sister I could get to strut with.

I wallowed in the wonderful sounds of "In the Mood," "Chattanooga Choo-Choo," "Tuxedo Junction," "Moonlight Serenade," and all those wonderful dance tunes.

I spent a wonderful hour before getting down to swatting, not even feeling a glimmer of guilt. But then it was head down and tail up, swatting like crazy.

When the exams were over, I felt confident I would get passes in all subjects, but how well, I would just have to wait until mid-January to find out.

First priority, however, was preparing for camp. It would be Neville, Laurie, Lynie, Middy, Bruce, and me—the same as had been sharing camps over three years. We knew each other so well, of course, that few secrets remained hidden in any breast. Including even Neville.

Neville, in fact, was to remain my longest friend from this group, even into our respective days not only of marriage, but of growing families.

This was to be a relaxing camp from the Friday afternoon train out to the Sunday evening train home. But still the same testing bushwalk with heavy packs containing everything we needed save fresh water. Preparing was routine by now, and after all the tensions of eight days of exams we were all ready to simply loll about on the beach and ride a breaker or two or three. All were reasonably competent bodysurfers by now, even the Schooner-shaped Middy.

It was a clever name that collectively over the years we had pulled together.

Ken Midson was indeed the school fat boy yet one never to shirk the exacting physical exercise of this hiking expedition. He declined the five-day hike the rest of us had done but never failed to join us on our two-day-two-night jaunts despite the steep descent and ascent. In New South Wales, the 'schooner' was the regular name for the large serve of beer in a pub, the fifteen-fluid-ounce glass, a well-rounded glass with no waist. The 'middy' was the ten-ounce glass, and only 'girlies' drank the modest 'pony.' Our Ken, nickname Middy, was indeed schooner-shape, so we felt no name, coined in jest, was more apt than 'Middy.' And it stuck for a while.

Many pastimes had been experienced both from our school camping trips and our many Boy Scout diversions, so we were never at a loss, if everybody felt like indulging, in mind games. We would play them by the hour, on occasions, as we either poked around in rock-pools looking for the deadly blue-ringed octopus or took nature-study walks over the headland to Era. Era was a more popularly attended beach than our favoured North Era because of its easier access—yet this attracted the families with kids, anyone preferring nudity. Unlike scout camps where large tents accommodated a dozen boys, the school camps were two-man 'pup' tents, so for conviviality after cleaning dinner dishes, our next several hours were spent sitting around a fire telling personal experiences.

Laurie, on this occasion, told the story of his young brother who, noticeably as he progressed from toddler stage, suffered some form of mental disorder. "No doctor or specialist would diagnose him as 'deficient,'" Laurie said, "but only last year a report was released giving the name 'autism' to conditions of children lacking desire to attach to others, even sometimes to parents. We noticed that my brother didn't like to be fussed over as most littlies do. He liked only his own company. He'd get upset if Mum even tried talking with him. Physically he is as healthy as any of us. And he's a bright little bugger, got a real sense of planning what he's about, but has his mind determinedly on only what he wants to do and how he goes about doing it. Mum thought he was just being naughty, but doctors decided it's his different way of looking at things. We simply cannot understand it. But there's no cure. And he won't start school. He insists on hiding from all other kids."

This led to Lynie talking about how his father, a doctor, was more than unhappy—in fact frustrated at there being so many diseases that medics had insufficient knowledge on. He was of the opinion that the war was likely advancing theories on both the physical body and the clinical mind.

Middy talked on his church, how his local vicar called the war God's way of teaching man to heed the lessons of the Bible—how discarding God's teaching can throw mankind into chaos. Ken didn't agree. He saw the vicar as narrow-minded, his opinion bordering on bigotry, and...

Oh, oh... we had to dive for the dictionary. But Nev always packed an abbreviated OED... "Never know, with boys your age when we start talking beyond social language, how often I'm called on to explain. And there can always be occasions, of course, when I'm not too sure, either."

So when we all knew what 'bigotry' meant, the tales continued. Within our tight circle, Middy's preparedness to talk on something as controversial as religion was understood, so when my turn came around I took a leaf from his book by talking about religion in my family.

"My stepfather is Roman Catholic. My father died five years ago, and Mum married again. We're Anglican. Mum and Pop never argue—they've simply seemed happy about everything. But there's a tension. To make him happy when they married, Mum changed to his religion so they could be married in a Catholic church and go to church together on Sundays. That was all right by my sister and me—we went to their Catholic wedding. Every Sunday morning since, when all are home, the four of us walk up Willoughby Road together to where the Catholic Church and the Anglican at Naremburn are across the road from each other. Mum and Pop go into their church, and Val and I into ours.

"Mum didn't want to get confirmed because she doesn't believe in confession, but Pop wanted it, so she did. Then when he wanted her to go to confession, she balked. I came home from school one day to find the head priest just coming out our gate—and as I came in the downstairs front door, I could hear Mum, upstairs, crying almost hysterically. 'He threatened me,' she sobbed, 'told me I would burn in purgatory the rest of my life, took me by the shoulders and shook me. He got so red in the face I thought he was going to hit me—I just screamed and told him to get out!'

"Mum firmly feels that confession is an intrusion on her personal life. Pop's trying to keep the peace on both sides, but the old priest won't give up, and it's causing ructions in what is otherwise a happy marriage. Sad but true."

Sixteen

Good news and bad news...

The good news was that on 12 November 1944 the Brits sank Germany's last remaining battleship.

The *Tirpitz* was sister ship to the *Bismarck*, operating out of Norwegian ports and creating havoc among merchant ships bringing supplies into Britain via the North Sea. Thirty-eight Lancaster bombers were assembled in Russia's northwest so they could approach the *Tirpitz* using the high Norwegian mountains as a radar screen. They pounded Germany's last remaining battleship with five-ton bombs. She keeled over to present the joyous airmen a view of her massive bottom.

More than a thousand German sailors died.

Does 'collateral damage' extend to the enemy? Or are Nazis simply 'victims'?

~ * ~

But can't good news ever get soured!

Bad news seemed to continue in waves.

The very next day we heard at breakfast that Glen Miller had gone missing in what could only have been a plane crash. And so it was found. He was killed, of course.

And the very next day, the *Wehrmacht* took advantage of a lull in fighting on the Western Front just as the Allies had actually crossed the German border. Winter snows in the top end of the world had bogged things down, and the Americans had dug in to wait while their supplies caught up. The German attacked with superior force, military and tanks, to drive the GIs back out of Germany. It was the first setback in months.

It was a massive counterattack catching the Americans napping. They'd run out of supplies. The Ardennes forest had been considered too thick for Jerry to think of attacking there, and snow was so thick that all aircraft were grounded.

"The Americans were taken completely by surprise," the wireless said. "*Panzer* tanks came charging through the forests. Allied forces are in retreat and suffering heavy losses."

And the *Panzer*, of course, was admitted even by MacArthur to be the most powerful tank in the entire war. So this was truly a significant setback. So much of the territory we had won with our now superior air power was conceded to the Germans as they pushed back through Holland and Belgium.

I had bought a really big map of Europe especially for following our drives into Germany. It was now showing me, oh so painfully, day by day, the several towns the Germans were retaking.

Oh those poor people living there! Only during the last weeks they had been gleefully greeting British and American saviours with garlands of flowers, to now be seeing the Germans return with guns blazing.

Oh how thankful I was that my exams were over. With this sort of war now raging, I would have been drawn into having to make dreadful decisions.

But at least the news from the Philippines, I confided with Ego, was good. General MacArthur declared the island of Leyte now completely in Allied hands and that landings were now being made on the main island of Luzon.

Oh what a mixed bundle of Christmas cheer.

Seventeen

1945

I'd had my eleventh birthday in Brisbane, twelfth in Sydney, thirteenth in Brisbane, fourteenth in Sydney, fifteenth in Brisbane and now sixteenth in Sydney. I was well and truly realising what people meant when they said they were well travelled. Whether or not all that broadened my mind I'm not sure, but I was known as the most travelled kid in North-Tech.

I liked to think it had broadened my mind, not only about places, but people—from the ticket office clerks I hoodwinked with white lies, to Ada and Elsie, the Snotty-Nose from Melbourne, Reecy and poor Edgar, and oh, not only so many brave soldiers on the trains but all those Gobs and GIs being so happily taken for a ride at Reecy's—those who didn't seem at all sad at having their lives turned upside down.

That January began my all but final year of school—two years of dedicated training to become the world's best architect. Well, that's the way I saw it.

Val had herself a serious boyfriend now—met him at the R&R club where she did voluntary work, a naval petty officer who, coincidentally, apart from being a Queenslander, also had sights on being an architect.

His early years of schooling for that were interrupted by the war, however.

Val had occasionally brought GIs and Gobs home for a Sunday dinner. She still worked with the American War Department and was still sworn to secrecy about what they did there. Her voluntary work was not now only at the Australian Servicemen's Club but also the American Servicemen's Club.

"The thing we miss more than anything when so far from home," they'd tell Mum, "is good old home cooking."

"Well, I don't know about home cooking in America," Mum would answer, "but I can offer you what we call 'good old home cooking' here." And she would plump down in front of them huge helpings of lamb that Pop had carved off the biggest leg the butcher had had that week, along with big scoops of gravy—and my mum made gravy that more than just wobbled, it ran all over the meat and tasted as good as it smelled. And there were piles of crispy roast spuds and pumpkin and greens. In the weeks they came on the Sunday, we then didn't have meat for a week because all the coupons had gone on the roast.

"But it's the least we can do for those boys," Mum said.

But when Val brought her Ian home for a second visit, and then a few months later, a third, we all felt "Oh-oh, this sure does look like it's getting serious."

"Maybe it's just Mum's cooking he comes for," I said one time, but Val gave me a not too playful clip on the ear.

And when it got to the stage of him staying over at our flat for a night or two, we knew it was serious. He'd got a promotion to sub-lieutenant along the way, so I reckoned he must have been good at his job. He was now a boss on PTs, little motor-torpedo boats. For two years he had operated along the coasts of New Guinea.

"Now we go further afield," is all he would tell me about where he operated now.

But he brought something of the war home one time. He was staying over, and he 'brought malaria.' I'd never seen someone with a malaria attack, but he had it bad. It was mid-January, height of summer and bloody hot, but he was shivering—his whole body shaking. We lit the Kosi stove, and he sat over it, wrapped in two blankets, but he still shivered. Val telephoned one of his shipmates, also on leave, and he had a military ambulance call and take Ian off to the naval hospital.

So here was yet another 'theatre of war' I'd experienced firsthand.

~ * ~

In the Ardennes, the German push declined as they literally ran themselves out of fuel to keep tanks and troops moving. German oil supplies were all but exhausted. Hitler's last valiant effort to retain some pride for Germany couldn't be sustained

It had been, right from the start, then, I realised, a desperate effort simply doomed to failure. But while I wouldn't dare admit it to Mum or Pop, or even to Laurie and Neville, I couldn't but help admire the German spirit in staging the counterattack. Many were killed in an exercise they knew could do no more than delay the inevitable. *Even the enemy can do brave deeds*, I couldn't help but think.

But on my big map, what still remained green was becoming thinner and thinner—in an east-to-west sense, that is. It was like a sandwich being squeezed between two great hands—a green sandwich. One hand was British tommies and American GIs squeezing from the west, the other the Russians, who even had women fighting alongside men in its armies, squeezing from the east.

The very next day the news was that Russia had overrun East Prussia, Germany's satellite state across the Polish corridor and was now within *cooee* of the main German border.

In Burma, British and Aussie forces had the Japs retreating.

Instead of the dour news of the last several years, the wireless was now giving more time to gut-twisting nostalgia: Vera Lynn's "We'll Meet Again" and new singers—well, new to me, anyway, like Billie Holliday, Bessie Smith, Frank Sinatra, Perry Como, Kate Smith, and Louis Armstrong... Oh, I could go on forever—I loved it all without demur, going to bed with dreams of Betty Grable and Diana Dorrs battling each other to be first into my bathtub with me.

~ * ~

Within a month of New Year, the Allies were across the French border into Germany itself. Oh what celebrations this brought!

At North-Tech, masters still had to change classrooms after each period according to what specialised subjects we had chosen for our two final years, and seemingly without fail for that entire day the incoming master's first words were, "Did you hear the good news this morning?"

We got to the stage of chorusing, "No, sir, what news is that?" to then watch him back down, realising, as the day wore on, how trite a question it was becoming. It was all done in good fun, of course, and all masters joined in the frivolity.

And the good news continued. When February was but two weeks old, we held all of Germany west of the Rhine. The Germans were too busy blowing up their own bridges to even try preventing our boys reaching that barrier.

In March, the Americans captured Manila, capital of the Philippines. General MacArthur had said back in 1942 when driven out that he would return... Well, now he had! It was a pretty horrific sort of battle because the Japs corralled all the locals into the last bastion they held, reckoning the Yanks wouldn't fire on them—but the Yanks did.

"War is war," MacArthur told those who said he shouldn't have. And I guess he had a point. Had he not opened fire, the Japs would have held out until those people starved to death anyway. And it would have set a precedent for the Japs to resort to in every major battle. So in my book, MacArthur, taking the hard decision, was right.

Wresting island after island from the Japs, however, had turned the war into a battle for snipers. Japs had to be dislodged from every building in turn. The longer that sort of battle went on, of course, the more casualties on both sides. We didn't mind how many Japs died, but our own boys' lives were precious. Every one was son or husband of someone at home where it was safe, as Mum and Pop kept reminding me.

Iwo Jima was a part of Japan, albeit an isolated island not too far from the Marshall and Caroline Islands that US forces had freed, and the heaviest hand-to-hand battle of the war was taking place there. The Japs defended it frantically, refusing to surrender. Six thousand Americans died—a dreadful setback to hopes of ending the Pacific War quickly. Dreadfully high losses of soldiers brave enough to make one beach assault after another despite seeing so many of their mates killed seemed a likely future to last whilst ever one Jap soldier remained. Japanese losses were always heavier than ours—but that didn't make the number of our dead easier to cope with.

In Europe, we quickly occupied the Ruhr Valley, Germany's industrial heartland. When our boys saw the devastation of large cities like Düsseldorf, Essen, and Dortmund that had been ruthlessly bombed by the Allies for months past, they were amazed. In entire cities, few buildings remained whole.

No wonder the German war effort was grinding to a halt, we were told at school—Germany could have no factories left!

On the Eastern Front, the Russians entered Vienna.

If I had thought a month ago that Europe was a shrinking green sandwich being nibbled away from both sides, it was now Germany itself starting to look thinner and thinner. I was having to change colours daily.

That the entire continent of Europe fitted comfortably inside a map of Australia, both at the same scale, had been a fact illustrated years ago in geography class. I wasn't taking geography or history any more because we had to choose, subject to career aspirations, a limited number of subjects. But the war had kept me pretty well informed of geography more or less throughout the world. What had started off with just Europe had so quickly become global. My education regarding nations, names, and neighbours was now extensive. But to look now at how Europe was so quickly changing, and to overlay that map, say, on the Sydney to Brisbane area, a part of geography I had travelled extensively by ship, motor car, and train, I was newly astounded... Australia had multi-miles of nothing in areas that in Europe comprised a dozen major cities with populations of millions compared to a nothing-ness!

It made one think, all right.

After the fall of the Philippines, we all hoped against hope that this meant the Japanese were at last finished, that they now realised their game was up and would surrender. But it wasn't to be.

"They will never surrender," said General MacArthur. "They will fight to the last man, woman, and child."

Hitler had already reached that stage. *The Sydney Morning Herald* was publishing pictures of German soldiers, captured as Germany made last-ditch stands, turning out to be fourteen and fifteen years old! Even younger than me!

~ * ~

In April the Soviet army swept into Berlin. Wow!

If I'd thought the photographs of the Ruhr Basin cities illustrated absolute devastation, the German capital was a wasteland of destruction. Wow again! In all the pictures, there didn't seem to be a whole building.

The German people who had been so cocksure of themselves when back in 1939 and 1940 country after country was surrendering to them, were now themselves skeletal from starvation. Children were scouring rubbish dumps and bombed-out buildings, searching for any scrap. Homes and contents of most were utterly destroyed, so all were as ill clad as hungry.

Could they even feel thankful that it was summer approaching rather than winter? Or were all, by now, so utterly cowed that they cared about nowt other than finding some crust of bread or a can of food missed by earlier scavengers?

I saw in a newsman's report that families were eating their own pets.

On April 29, German forces still in Italy surrendered.

On April 30, Hitler suicided.

Admiral Doenitz was given charge of Germany, and on May 5 he announced surrender of all German forces.

~ * ~

For the British man and woman in the street, the war was over.

The dreadful bombing of Britain when parts of London were laid as much to waste as the now state of Berlin, their tragic losses of sons and lovers, and their years of hunger were past. They could now bring home the young sons and daughters that had been evacuated during the dreadful years of German bombing, from countries like Australia, New Zealand, South Africa, and Canada.

I even knew some of them. Hadn't my own Aunt Moogs and Uncle Lance taken in two girls from England, raised them during the war years as their own? Hadn't I known boys at school who remembered sleeping under London staircases every night because 'under-stairs' was the safest place in a house against collapsing roofs?

From today, those families could again look with some hope towards a future.

"But we've still the Pacific War to win," insisted our newspapers. "Nippon is yet unbowed."

I pinned that up on my bedroom wall so it was the first thing my eyes would fall on each morning.

No, we dare not yet start to sit back, I told Ego.

Of course we didn't yet know about Darwin. We knew our only city in our country's north had been bombed, but we hadn't been told that it had been practically razed to the ground as devastatingly as Berlin. Japanese bombers had not, fortunately, ever been able to reach other Aussie cities.

However, there was great personal news for me.

At Scouts in early May, they told me my application for King Scout recognition was approved! I qualified! A King's Scout lanyard was to be added to my uniform.

Twenty-three badges on my sleeves qualified me in each of the categories *Personal Growth, Adventurous Activities, Community Involvement* and *Leadership Qualities.*

Oh, the thrill of that! I grew to ten feet tall that night.

"Hey, look at this," I announced over dinner next night, showing the assembled family the letter from Government House in Canberra. It read:

> ...the presentation will be made by His Royal Highness Prince Henry William Frederick Albert, Duke of Gloucester, Earl of Ulster and Baron Culloden, Governor-General of Australia, KG, KT, KP, GCB, GCMG, GCVO.

"... Now what do you reckon about that?"

I didn't simply feel ten feet tall; I felt I was perched atop the highest pedestal in the land.

Pop took the letter and scanned through the rest.

"Ah," he said, "it's to be on 24 May, British Empire Day. Quite appropriate. But, my boy, whilst the governor-general is the King's personal representative, this doesn't mean he will make the presentation personally. He will likely be represented by someone from the NSW governor's office in Sydney. So don't be disappointed if that happens. On Empire Day, I would imagine the duke will have official functions to attend in Canberra."

But I wasn't going to be disappointed. I was already on top of the world.

Every Empire Day the Scouts were on parade at the Trooping of the Colour or whatever they called the ceremony at the Sydney Sports Ground. And the state governor was always there to give a speech. So yes, it was highly likely Pop was right.

And it happened that way. Mum made a special job of ironing my tunic and I double-polished my shoes. First Chatswood was given a front post in the parade, and I was called up to the podium, where the governor, an old geyser with a wrinkly face, draped the lanyard, all red and white striped, around my neck, across my chest, looping it through my epaulette so its tassel fell across my heart.

I felt especially proud when the governor announced that I was one of only eight King Scouts in all New South Wales.

Well, did I feel great? Or what?

Eighteen

June 1945

India and Burma were free of Japanese troops. Those not killed had retreated into Thailand.

When the Japanese began invading nations to their south, any not agreeing to give Japanese forces unhindered access through their territories to invade British colonies were themselves invaded and subjugated. When it was Thailand's turn to answer the question, it sensibly agreed in order to retain its sovereignty. Japan made free of its territory, however, and prevailed on Thailand to let it build a railroad through its western territory, using prisoners of war as free labour, to invade Burma and India.

Now, with the reversal of war fortunes, Japan was on the run from territories captured.

The Pacific Western Front was won. Britons, Aussies, Canadian, and Chinese forces had retaken Burma, and the Japs were licking wounds as they fled through Thailand to protect their still-captive colonies of Cambodia, Laos, and Vietnam.

The Pacific Eastern Front was also being won. US forces had retaken the Marshall and Caroline Islands and now completed their capture, at a great cost in lives, however, of Iwo Jima, the first Japanese home island to fall into Allied hands.

The Pacific Southern Front was pushing northwards. Australian and Dutch forces were retaking the many islands of the Dutch East Indies, and the United States had the Philippines almost totally reclaimed.

~ * ~

Okinawa, Japan's major island of the Ryuku group, her southernmost territory, was the next obvious target. It was essential to have such a base if the United States were to bomb Japan's home islands into submission. Whilst Japan's fleet had been decimated, the cost to the United States was that too few aircraft carriers to mount sustained bombing raids on Japan's industrial resources were left.

GIs had landed on Okinawa three months since and were meeting horrendous opposition. They were taking to Japanese dugouts with flame-throwers, the most inhuman type of warfare imaginable, although essential, the wireless reckoned, when the suicidal Japanese demanded thousands of Allied lives in exchange for even an acre of ground. So progress continued slow and life-costly.

The battle of Okinawa was the largest amphibious assault in the Pacific War, and it took three months of fighting, with horrendous losses before the United States could claim the island as taken. Okinawa had the highest number of casualties of any World War Two engagement. Japanese losses were more than fifty thousand troops and a hundred thousand civilians, many of which were suicides. The United States lost twelve thousand men.

~ * ~

In Europe, horrific slaughter of a different nature was being realised.

Germany's Death Camps were being discovered in the thinning green sandwich by Russians in the east and British and Americans in the west. At first it was thought the camps, over which the stink of death hovered in sickening clouds, were for prisoners of war, but it quickly became apparent that they were civilians—Jewish civilians, men, women, and children—breathing skeletons all.

Oh, how I wished I were there, a soldier with a gun in my hands so I could search out the frightened Nazi guards hiding in corners as those camps were captured. I wouldn't shoot them, however, well not to bring quick death, anyway—maybe just a bullet in each knee then one in the groin so they could slowly bleed to death—or maybe hanging them by their testicles with tight wire nooses as they roasted over hot coals? It was a time for letting imagination run high.

Newspapers were daily giving us double-page spreads of the poor victims, those not yet fed to the huge ovens especially built to dispose of their bodies once gassed, yet already near death from forced labour and starvation.

One night I actually woke up with my stomach in such a roil that I'd filled my bed with vomit. Mum threatened to stop me seeing newspapers in future. Yet she didn't. She knew if she forbade me that I'd only be tempted to find a sneaky way of seeing them. Auschwitz, Buchenwald, Dachau, and many more were names to live in infamy for evermore.

~ * ~

So much was happening so quickly in the war that I was now bringing my atlas to the breakfast table. I had flagged the pages showing what had been Germany and the best map of the Western Pacific so I could quickly turn pages as the newsreader spoke.

Oh, what a dilemma the Pacific War was turning out to be.

Was every square inch of Japan going to be as costly as taking Iwo Jima and Okinawa?

What seemed inevitable, if we were to defeat Japan, was that not hundreds of thousands of Allied servicemen were yet to die, but millions!

How could there be a final *coup de grace* as there was in Europe, when Japanese would indeed fight to their very death rather than surrender?

~ * ~

American 'Flying Fortresses,' biggest bombers in the world, with now bases close enough for daily bombing the Japanese homelands, the factories that manufactured armaments, tanks, and planes, were day by day reducing Japanese cities to the rubble that Germany had become. At sea, with the Japanese fleet decimated, American and Australian submarines were sinking every ship endeavouring to approach Japanese ports.

So we're going to starve the Japanese out, I told Ego. *We know they cannot grow enough of their own food. This was one of the very reasons they started the war!*

Nineteen

15 August 1945

When Mousy burst into our English class one day, without knocking, it caused a furore. It was simply not done for anyone, master or not, to burst into a classroom interrupting whatever the proceedings. We'd nicknamed him Mousy years ago because not only was he the only master in the school to still insist on wearing a cloak and mortarboard, but he illustrated all the characteristics of stature and sneakiness of a highly stressed mouse. He taught mathematics, and when afternoon sunbeams cast long shadows onto the blackboard when he had his back to us, the shadow cast by the mortarboard looked, for all the world, like extended ears. And he really was quite diminutive in stature and moved in short, sharp bursts as if hovering at each corner to see if a lump of cheese lay somewhere accessible. And he had a squeaky voice, so Mousy seemed a derogatory enough designation to do him the justice we felt he deserved.

"The war is over," he squeaked at his highest possible decibel. "It just came in over the radio. Japan has surrendered."

Well! But it only took a minute before the entire class began cheering, jumping about, all the boys hugging each other. Mousy ran to our English master, and those two clasped each other almost passionately and began jigging around as excitedly as us kids.

Just a few days prior we had had the news that the United States had dropped on Hiroshima, the city near Tokyo that housed Japan's major military establishments, the newest and most secret of weapons, what they called an atomic bomb. Well, did it ever wipe that city off the map! The photos for the next several days certainly illustrated an even greater desolation of a metropolis than ever London or Berlin could claim. And seventy-two hours later, they dropped another on Nagasaki, Japan's greatest industrial city after Tokyo.

"If you don't surrender now," the Allies declared to Japan's Royal Palace, "our next target is Tokyo."

Well, did that ever bring results! What more proof could you ask, that actions do indeed speak louder than words?

Or, if you were to ask me, I'd say, "Well, at least more meaningfully."

Some wag in the class jumped on to his desk with his exercise book and began tearing it into shreds and tossing the pieces into the air like confetti. And the rest followed suit. And the masters didn't seem to mind.

Very soon, not only did the bell begin to toll in the school bell tower, but the 'all clear' air raid signal began its wail from seemingly all over Sydney. Soon car horns could be heard toot-toot-tooting with reckless abandon as well as every horn aboard every ship in the harbour.

Who was it said that while bad news of the war took an age to reach us, good news arrived excitingly fast?

Well, it was certainly true now. Laurie and I danced along with all the other boys, every soul in sight screaming with glee.

Up went a shout: "Hey, how about getting into the city? Celebrations will be wild over the harbour!"

North-Tech was situated right across the street from North Sydney train station, trains from there going direct onto the Harbour Bridge. Also trams. City centre was only the other end of the bridge. We couldn't be closer without already being there.

We didn't even wait for school to be declared over; we simply left school bags and all to dash from class, from school, across the road to the station. Already boys from Shore School were arriving there. And there was a 'helluva' queue at the public phones. But Laurie and I dutifully queued up, each spending tuppence to phone our mums. Pop answered our phone, and I asked if it was all right to go with my mates into the city, and he said, "Of course, so long as you promise, no alcohol."

I promised.

We didn't even wait for the next train to arrive but were back up onto the street for a tram.

And nobody was collecting fares. The conductor was up front, an arm around the driver's shoulder. They were having their own celebration.

I hadn't realised a tram could hold so many kids—we hung from doors and all along the footplate the guard used when taking fares.

Across the bridge, there were so many trams queued up in the tunnel at the city end that we couldn't get all the way to the terminus. We simply joined those on foot squeezing past the stationery tramcars.

And when we gained the street, what chaos!

People were going wild. Trams were halted because people blocked the streets. Loudspeakers mounted throughout the city to assist with crowd control in case of air raids were already, instead of trying to control crowds, blaring out "Jumpin'-Jive" from Glen Miller, Woody Herman, Dizzy Gillespie—it was all honky-tonk, rag-mop, and boogie-woogie rolled into one. Shufflin' Shoes wasn't even close!

Where did they get all this music together so quickly? How did they know there was going to be this party?

But I wasn't looking for answers. I lost Laurie within minutes of gaining the street. It just wasn't possible to keep together. It was just a matter of boy grabbing girl or vice versa, or several, and joining the party.

Wow, did I ever appreciate learning jive at the Scout Hall dances—I simply lost track of time and what was going on.

Whatever happened to inhibition?

I recall being on one motor car going anywhere, but never fast, for there was too much of a crush aboard it, but all car horns were seemingly stuck on "On," and even when I left it I still had no idea what sort of car it was or who might have been driving it—if anybody. How the hell could they see? Bodies were clinging all over it, so many bodies I couldn't count—twenty? thirty? It was simply a case of finding a toehold and hands to grip onto for as long as you could before falling off or hearing more music you couldn't resist.

I never drank, and I got home by train. Trams were still hopelessly stuck in the tunnel, so I caught a train and walked the several blocks from St. Leonards—also free.

~ * ~

Mum and Pop were as jubilant, even if not expressing it as physically as me. And Val was in happy tears because her sailor-boy would now be safe from such serious danger as scraps with Jap submarines and assisting the Yanks in beach assaults.

Within a month, the Allies formed a United Nations pact.

But will it have more teeth than the League of Nations formed after the First World War? I asked Ego. But he had no measure either. Only time could answer.

By now, I was old enough to look at things cynically. I realised I had a cynical streak only when Aunt Wyn told me so. She could tell after our first coaching session—a getting-to-know-each-other hour.

"You've a real cynical steak in you," she told me with a grin.

Wyn was the wife of Ken, my Uncle Harold's 'nephew that might be his son.' It had been arranged in that me wanting to sit for honours degrees in three Leaving Certificate subjects come end of 1946, I should now, at end of 1945, sit with them for a briefing session so they had time to assess standards and establish a programme.

I was seeking honours in English, Maths-1, and Maths-2. Uncle Harold had offered to pay for coaching lessons and subbing my pocket money so I could quit working after school and instead come Mondays and Wednesdays to Wyn and Ken's house in Mosman. Wyn was a retired, though still young enough to have young sons to rear, high school history and English teacher. She would coach me in English, two hours each of two afternoons a week, I would have dinner with them those nights, and Ken would coach me after dinner in two hours in maths. I could ride my bike there with no problem. It meant changing my Gran's shopping day from Wednesday to Tuesday, but that didn't worry her, and I was still free, then, for Scouts on Tuesday nights

But, wow! An entire year of homework to be completed for not only my final year at North-Tech but also for homework set from time to time by Wyn and Ken.

The high school English curriculum was like second nature for Wyn, of course. I found she could even 'pitch' pretty accurately what exam questions I was likely to face each term. She was particularly happy that *Hamlet* was my compulsory Shakespeare study for the year, because it was her favourite.

"Its character studies make it a challenging joy," she insisted, "quite apart from being his best-illustrated command of Elizabethan English."

And Mum and Pop were pretty good. Mum had her unique way, of course, of really putting me on the spot when wanting something out of me. "Inside that door, my lad," she would say, pointing to my room where I did my study and homework in private. "You are on an honour basis to study and not waste time on things like your balsa modelling or Scouting studies. I can tell when you're lying, of course"—which she indeed had an uncanny knack of doing—"so I'll keep asking if you're being honest about it."

So what else could a bloke do when chucked a challenge like that? No punches, it was just a case of "Do it or bloody else!"

"You have a lot of people depending on you to respond," she would add to further drive in the barbs, " Harold and Wyn and Ken, to say nowt of Pop and me."

So a bloke had to really knuckle down when you knew she always turned out to be right about things. And I did knuckle down, once having got her agreement that all through Christmas and for the first two weeks of January I could spend at the pool.

"Mid-January is the New South Wales Championships, before school starts—and you know how important this year is for me—last chance to take a place."

"I'm glad you didn't say 'first place.' You know how disappointed you were last year when missing out. It wouldn't be a good start to your academic studies to feel you failed at that. Make sure you settle on 'a place' and not 'first place.'"

A kid can't win, you know. She's always that one bloody jump ahead.

~ * ~

Christmas slid past so quickly, it being the only day that week that I didn't spend in the pool. Who should turn up to see me swim when the finals came up? Not only Mum, Pop, and Val but Uncle Harold, Wyn and Ken, and Desolie, my 'adopted' sister from Northbridge. I knew my immediate family was coming of course, but spied the others only when on the podium...

And yes. Oh what a way to start a New Year! I got my Blue! I can never claim it to be a clear-cut victory, however, because when the sprint finished I still didn't know if I'd won. Being a 'left-side-only' breather, the only way I could see during the race how I was placed with swimmers in lanes on my right was when my face was underwater, and I knew that during the last two strokes I could lose an inch by trying to see too far to my right. I just had to stop myself from looking.

That inch is too important, Ric, Ego kept shouting. *...concentrate on only speed during every fraction of every second.*

And dear Ego had been right as he ever was. I knew I had the two kids to my left beaten, because I could see them each time I breathed, but of the five to my right I knew only that the my immediate neighbour, from Fort Street High, was right with me, so much so that I didn't know whether that fraction of an inch favoured me or him, or if someone to his right was further ahead still. And where the three swimmers even further on my right were I had no idea at all.

I didn't even turn to breathe coming up that last stroke. To save a further fraction of an inch, I'd rather my lungs burst.

They didn't. But when my head surfaced once my finger touched the tile, three other heads were also coming up, trying to shake water out of their eyes to see who touched first. But there's no way of knowing of course, until it comes up on the screen—and it was a terribly long several seconds before that happened.

I'd won by a half second. When that '3' came up, I felt my heart do double flips.

The North-Tech benches went wild—nearly as wild as my heart, still beating so fast and hard it was a great thumping in my chest that lasted right through the presentation. I never was able to remember the walk back to the dressing-room and showers.

And I was smothered by the family, of course, when joining them. But I stayed with them only a few seconds before going to sit with the school.

Now I knew how Winston Churchill and General MacArthur felt, having won the war.

~ * ~

Back at the start of school the next week, for my final year, all exuberance over the win, such wonderful relief after all the years of looking towards that event, was quickly pushed down the list of life priorities. Every subject master cautioned us when welcoming us that this was crunch year in our education.

"Whether you hope to pass for university at the end of this year or simply equip yourself for the best possible job to start out on your life's career, this is time to put the exuberance of youth on the shelf and knuckle down to 'serious bloody study.'"

Val's Ian was great inspiration. On being demobbed, he applied for admission to Sydney Uni's School of Architecture. He, with mates, took especially provided lodgings for returning servicemen on the North Shore campus, not far from Crow's Nest. So he became a regular visitor and gave me lots of hints about his college training before the war.

The trigonometry area of Maths-2 coupled with tech drawing were the essential subjects in gaining admittance. English and Math-1 were my other subjects. French, history, geography, physics, and science had gone by the board. I had only my four best subjects to concentrate on. Physics and science had always been my weakest subjects; I would miss French because I had enjoyed studying a foreign language, but it was no longer essential in my career path.

In history of the world and geography, I realised how lucky I had been in so closely following all aspects of the war. Those five or more years taught me more about those subjects than any kid had ever learned during any other period. Later in life I might well, if fortune went my way, make more use of both those subjects, and the French, in whatever form I could fit them in with my main career path. I knew only that I had a burning desire to see all those places my atlas had introduced me to, and to meet the people of those lands.

However, my seventeenth year of life on this earth was destined to be one of head down and tail up.

Twenty

January 1948

The Second World War might be over, but my personal war was just beginning.

I turned eighteen just a week before exam results were published. Had the war not finished, I would, by now, have been conscripted to fight in it. However, fighting a war I certainly found myself.

I gained my honours in English and Maths-2, but had to be content with only an A-level in Maths-1. And I was happily mentioned in the New South Wales Education Department's 'short-list' as having come second in the state in my entrance exam to Sydney University's School of Architecture. So all that was good-stuff—personal achievements as exciting, say, as having become a King's Scout or winning a State Blue in Swimming.

Yet not all was good. I was instead informed that for the second year, all places in the School of Architecture were taken by returning servicemen...

School-leavers are required to submit applications again between 1st and 15th November next, for 1949.

Oh dear.

I appealed, my mother and stepfather appealed, my Uncle Harold, an industry leader with an ear to cabinet minsters, also appealed.

"Surely the number of places can be increased by, say, three only, that the three most impressive students can be admitted, which would inconvenience no additional returning servicemen," they claimed. But to no avail. The department stood firm.

~ * ~

My application was re-submitted on 1 November as recommended. In January 1949 I received by mail, the department's response:

> *We regret to inform that all places in the School of Architecture are again being taken by returning servicemen. School-leavers 1947 and 1948 are required to submit applications again between 1st and 15th November next, for 1950.*

~ * ~

Somehow I had to learn to put disappointment behind me.

Enquiries to the department as to how many returning servicemen were still on the list to enter university brought no helpful response.

Enquiries as to why, in the circumstance, intake numbers could not be increased proved as futile.

Succumbing to depression after all the support given to our war effort, albeit moral support, is for Aussies surely only less determined than you, insisted Ego. And he was right again, of course.

Yet it did seem somewhat ironic, a peacetime government insisting I surrender rather than keep fighting. During wartime, such surrender would have been considered treason.

Epilogue

After the war it was discovered that it had been agreed by Australia's government and military chiefs that if the Japanese had landed troops in the country, the only defensive line to be mounted was the Boomerang Coast—the stretch of coastline from Brisbane in the north to Melbourne in the south and west sixty miles to the Great Dividing Range. The rest must be sacrificed.

Even to attempt defending the Boomerang Coast, it was admitted, could at best, only prove a futile gesture.

The war taught Australia that it had to populate or, in the event of any other such threat, perish. Australia opened its doors to immigration by displaced persons from all Allied European countries. It was a decision to change the country from an insular majority to one of the most forward-looking, multi-cultural societies in the world.

The third Japanese mini-submarine sighted in Sydney Harbour in 1942 was discovered by fishermen in August 2006 in seventy fathoms of ocean off Sydney's northern beaches. It had obviously been crippled by depth charges, yet able to quit the harbour and head north. It succumbed to its injuries before getting twenty miles

Mum and Lou Somers lived happily until Lou's death seven years after marriage. Mum later remarried; when she buried her third husband, Val and I nicknamed her 'Lucretia.'

Valerie married her Ian Black, who was to have a distinguished career in architecture. The entire township of Mt. Isa, built to support the discovery of the world's greatest copper deposits, was one of his achievements before succumbing to a brain tumour at the unfortunate early age of forty, same as Dad.

Desolie Richardson, my 'adopted' sister, became a successful businesswoman. She travelled the world promoting the world-renowned Berlie-Bra. She became a director of Berlie-Hestia and was, at her peak, named among the ten most highly paid women in Australian Industry. In later life, she married the company founder, Sir John Hurley, to become Desolie Lady Hurley. For many years she was Patron of the Australian Girl Guides Association and the New South Wales YWCA. She was also instrumental in promoting many national charities.

Uncle Harold's personal contribution to satisfying inner needs saw him rise to the chair of Grand Master of NSW's Grand Lodge of Freemasonry.

More than can be told in words is that my first wife and I were, for three years after our marriage in 1951, jitterbug-jive champions of our local Sydney 'hop.' After being widowed with two young children, I married again, and Maggie and I, during my 'alternative' career, travelled the world extensively. We divorced after twenty years, since which time I really cashed in on what I learned from the war. The following bio touches on the detail.

~ * ~

I've enjoyed writing this little background on the war.

I had never intended writing a biography of any sort, yet when recently watching some television it dawned on me how it was the war that sparked so many of the goals that influenced my life. It seemed so many of the lines I traced from my atlas in those years became paths to be later traversed not only by my feet, but my mind.

Meet Kev Richardson

Following a career in business management at international level, Kev attained a degree in journalism, to then sweat as far up the River Nile as one can get, canoe down the Amazon, flash countless photographs from atop the Eiffel Tower, the heights above Yosemite, the Victoria Falls, *et al*, scream *"Ole!"* at a Chihuahua bullfight, ride elephant trails in Thai jungles, wallow in the incredible history of Rapa Nui's Maoi—and as convention almost demands, was mugged in Bogotá. His articles on travel to exotic lands have featured in travel and airline magazines around the world.

Meanwhile, being a sixth-generation descendant from Australia's First Fleet with an obsessive interest in his country's founding, he was disappointed at generations of suppression in the hidden truths of that history. Years of fact-finding, with the help of other dedicated researchers, revealed all, and Kev vowed to set the history books aright by bringing the truths of convictism to light. He is well qualified to do so, for as a student of First Fleet history, he has presented his subject on many occasions in press, radio, and television interviews. He is a past president of *The First Fleet Fellowship* and a past secretary of *The Descendants of Convicts Inc.* During Australia's 1988 Bicentenary he officiated in Founding celebrations in Sydney, Melbourne, Hobart, and Norfolk Island. For his work during that Bicentenary, he was created honorary life member of *The Regiment of Redcoat Descendants.*

Kev now devotes his life to writing on not only his country's convict history and general fiction with an Australian flavour, but biographies of significant people. He recognises the growing trend towards digital reading, so follows the world's top authors in publishing his works both as traditional paperbacks and the economical eBook.

His *Gurrewa* (two books in the series), *Brogan* (four books in the series) and his *Letitia Munro* trilogy, all released by *Wings-Press* (wingsepress.com), include awards-winners and five-star reviews. Synopses of all works can be read on www.kev-richardson.com. Three biographies are contracted for release during 2010.

These days Kev travels less, having retired from his home on Queensland's Gold Coast, left his grown family and friends, to write from experiences and adventures during his exciting travels, happily ensconced in the foothills of the Golden Triangle in amazing Thailand's exotic north.

Other Works From The Pen Of
Kev Richardson

Gurrewa – Finalist in the 2002 Independent eBook Awards. A true story of the shame of a nation's founding. It empties the vacuum cleaner after the Australian authorities of the day had swept the dust of truths under the carpet. Adam lives the shame of those days.

ADAM–Son of Gurrewa – A tale of discovery in New South Wales. The Children of convicts discover how Australia is indeed the lucky country. He helps lead it to its burgeoning wealth in both real and personal riches. Convict traits emerge to create unique personal attitudes in their new land.

Brogan - A tale of life on Australia's desert edge. In the early 1900s Australia was a nation in transition. Brogan, born in the drifting sands of the far outback, his life exemplifies the blood and guts characteristics by which Aussies are recognised even today.

Brogan's Bust – Brogan, enmeshed in intrigue, flies a courier service in the Amazonian jungles where graft and corruption make mockery of the law. Back-stabbing amongst cartel middle-men, goaded by greed, turn a hiccup into a stumble that generates into a fall to begin a slide that snowballs into an avalanche.

Brogan's Bella - Isabella and Brogan are victims in a deadly hijack. Their carefree trip through leisurely Pacific Islands becomes a nightmare of death and terror. Their holiday turns into a year of incarceration and intimidation, embroiled in the cut-throat intrigue of jungle politics and guerrilla warfare, or facing the cutting of their own throats for even knowing the truths behind the hijack.

Brogan Abroad – A modern Brogan finds himself embroiled in three simultaneous adventures, planning none yet finding each destines him to having his throat slit in some dark alley. *Yet what can a man do,* he laments, *when to accomplish one I must fail at another?* He juggles hiding in Thailand from a Sydney drug cartel with smuggling a high-profile prostitute into Australia as well as being hijacked in third-world Sudan as it counts down hours to bloody revolution.

Letitia Munro – A true tale of Australia's first white settlement—of those who in witless ignorance transform the world's biggest prison into a land of free enterprise and pride. Ignominy of servitude bred in them irrefragable support for underdogs, determination of purpose towards mateship and their flippant attitude to authority and class distinction.

To Plough Van Diemen's Land – Children of convicts spawn a new ethos. Titia's descendants, illiterate and utterly unskilled must learn everything by surviving hard knocks and bad luck. Some fail yet many succeed, converting empty pockets into acres of sheep as, on their frontiers, they remain unaware of the social taboos being woven into the nation's spawning culture.

The Terrible Truths - Third in the *Letitia Munro* trilogy finds the children and grandchildren swept up in the traumas of having to hide the truths of their heritage as society values change—and to as well begin coping with the growth of industry beginning to shake the world's economies. Australia begins emerging as a veritable beehive of mines as minerals of every description begin bringing riches to the land.

An Epic Life (August 2010) – True tale of adventurous people reaching across the world to fulfil dreams—a major achievement in the nineteenth century. The Steam Railway revolutionises time and travel, the industrial revolution catapults Britain into the world's most powerful nation. Two couples from different lifestyles whisk their very lives into a froth and bubble existence to create, on the far side of the world, a Dynasty.

Gerard Rawes (November 2010) – Gerard finds his life transformed from rags to riches. He discovers how circumstances can pluck a man from one situation and drop him in another—as a tsunami can pluck a body from a beach and seemingly cast him up on the shore of distant world. In England's mid-eighteenth century, the emerging industrial revolution catapults Gerard out of a world of serfdom into London's elite—a true-life biography.

Letter to Our Readers

Enjoy this book?

You can make a difference

As an independent publisher, Wings ePress, Inc. does not have the financial clout of the large New York Publishers. We can't afford large magazine spreads or subway posters to tell people about our quality books.

But, we do have something much more effective and powerful than ads. We have a large base of loyal readers.

Honest Reviews help bring the attention of new readers to our books.

If you enjoyed this book, we would appreciate it if you would spend a few minutes posting a review on the site where you purchased this book or on the Wings ePress, Inc. webpages at: https://wingsepress. com/

Visit Our Website

For The Full Inventory
Of Quality Books:

Wings ePress.Inc
https://wingsepress.com/

Quality trade paperbacks and downloads
in multiple formats,
in genres ranging from light romantic comedy
to general fiction and horror.
Wings has something for every reader's taste.
Visit the website, then bookmark it.
We add new titles each month!

Wings ePress Inc.

3000 N. Rock Road

Newton, KS 67114

www.ingramcontent.com/pod-product-compliance
Lightning Source LLC
Chambersburg PA
CBHW070302120726

47910CB00007B/2350